The Great Big Book of Rhythm

By "Miss Jackie" Weissman

FROM THE AUTHOR

THE IDEAS in "The Great Big Book of Rhythm" were developed over many years of working with parents, teachers and, of course, children.

RHYTHM IS a very important element in the education of young children. Through rhythm activities, children begin to sense the concepts of order, organization and discipline, freeing them to be creative.

YOU DO NOT HAVE TO BE A MUSICIAN TO USE THE IDEAS IN THIS BOOK! Most of the ideas are simple rhythm games and each page of this book is a self-contained lesson.

SOME OF the material in "The Great Big Book of Rhythm" was developed for two of my earlier books, "Hello, Rhythm" and "Hello, Sound." This material has been completely rewritten and revised, however. A special note of thanks goes to Editor Extraordinaire Jerry Maloney, without whose assistance this book would have been much more difficult to write.

THE IDEAS in this book can be useful in a classroom setting, for youth groups, camps, preschools or nurseries. The activities will develop listening, language, cognitive and motor skills—which, in turn, develop self-concept and self-esteem.

HAPPY RHYTHM!

Miss Jackie

TABLE OF CONTENTS

RHYTHM IN LANGUAGE

RHYTHM EXPERIENCES develop language in young children. Singing, in particular, plays an important role in language development—when you sing, you put vowels and consonants in a rhythmic order.

OVER THE YEARS I have worked with thousands of parents and children, using music. The majority of the parents have always told me that they feel their child's language development was enhanced by the musical experiences.

RHYTHM ALL OVER

PURPOSE—*Listening for rhythm patterns.*

CHILDREN LIKE to say new words. I've seen children repeat the same word over and over, simply because they enjoy saying it. Rhythm begins with speech patterns, followed later by other parts of the body.

TEACHER SAYS, "A word I like to say is 'ice cream.' Can you say that with your mouth? Can you say that with with your hands"? *(Clap hands to syllables.)* "Can you say that with your head?" *(Move head up and down in syllables.)* "Another word I like to say is 'spaghetti.' Can you say that with your mouth? Can you say that with your feet?" *(Stamp feet to syllables.)* "Can you say that with your eyes?" *(Blink eyes to syllables.)*

ASK THE children what words they like to say. Ask about specific subjects —for example, "What do you like to eat?" Some answers might be peanut butter, lollipops, marshmallows, milk, etc.

LET ONE of the children pick out his or her favorite word and tell that word to the class. Now, the class has to say the word—with mouth, hands, feet, eyes, etc. (This exercise goes with the song "I've Got a Rhythm" on page 86.)

HAVE THE class do rhythm to entire sentences. This will help them understand the concepts of fast and slow. "Let's all go out to play." *(Clap hands to syllables.)* "I hope I have ice cream for dinner." *(Pat thighs to syllables.)* "Tomorrow is Christmas Eve." *(Stamp feet to syllables.)*

BYE BYE BABY

Appalachian
Traditional

Bye, bye,— ba - by ba - by, bye:

My lit - tle ba - by ba - by bye.

Bye, bye,— ba - by, ba - by bye:

My lit - tle ba - by, ba - by, bye.

Dye Dye Daby
Fye Fye Faby
Gye Gye Gaby
Hye Hye Haby
Jye Jye Jaby
Kye Kye Kaby
Etc.

BYE, BYE, BABY

PURPOSE—*Language development.*

LULLABIES ARE common to every culture. Parents all over the world seem to have an innate ability to spontaneously create lullabies to soothe their babies. Lullabies are simply soothing, rhythmic, repetitive sounds sung with feeling. "Bye, Bye, Baby" is an old, old lullaby from Virginia's Appalachian Mountain region. There is no known composer. The song just "was there."

SING "Bye, Bye, Baby" to the children. Soon they'll be singing along. Have them cradle a "baby" while they sing.

AFTER YOU have sung the song with the children, try changing the beginning sounds of the words. For example:

> Sye, sye, saby, saby, sye,
> My little saby, saby, sye,
> Sye, sye, saby, saby, sye,
> My little saby, saby, sye.

LULLABIES ARE perfect for closing out the school day. The children will relax and go home feeling satisfied.

A RHYTHM ROUND

PURPOSE—*Total rhythm involvement.*

THIS GAME can be played with any age group and adapted to any subject. It's also fun to play! Young children love it. As an example, we'll use July 4 as our subject.

THE TEACHER creates a discussion about the Fourth of July. Why is this day important to the USA? What do we celebrate? The purpose of this discussion is to elicit vocabulary words that can be used in our rhythm rhyme. For example:

> What do we celebrate on July 4? (Our freedom)
> What do many people put up on July 4? (Flags)
> What do many families do on July 4? (Picnic)
> How many states does our country have? (Fifty)

WHEN YOU have enough feedback, select four words about the Fourth of July—freedom, flag, picnic, fifty.

NOW, HAVE a "rhythm round." (A round is a musical form wherein several groups sing different parts of a song at the same time. "Row, Row, Row Your Boat" is a good example.) Divide the class into four groups. Each group is assigned a word to be repeated four times.

Group One—Freedom, freedom, freedom, freedom.
Group Two—Flag, flag, flag, flag.
Group Three—Picnic, picnic, picnic, picnic.
Group Four—Fifty, fifty, fifty, fifty.

AFTER THE children have practiced until they know their parts, the game begins. Group One begins by saying "freedom" four times, over and over. Group Two starts after the first group has said "freedom" the first four times. Group Two says "flag" four times, then Group Three starts while the others keep going. ONCE YOU START, DON'T STOP! Group Four begins when Group Three has said "picnic, picnic, picnic, picnic" four times. When all four groups are going at the same time, satisfaction will be very high.

THE USE OF rhythm instruments will add a nice touch to this exercise. (Note: with children under four years old, it's best to start with only two groups.)

YOUR NAME IS A RHYTHM

PURPOSE—*Recognizing and comparing the same and different rhythms.*

EACH CHILD in your class is very special, with his or her own rhythm. Tell the children they are going to discover their very own rhythms today.

TEACHER—"My name is _____. I'm going to clap my name." *(Clap your hands on each syllable of your name.)* "What's your name?"

CHILD—"Mary Weston."

TEACHER—"Let's say Mary's name: Ma-ry Wes-ton. Now, let's clap Mary's name." *(Clap the syllables, then turn to the next child.)* "What's your name?"

CHILD—"Tony Semolino."

TEACHER—"Let's say Tony's name. To-ny Sem-o-lin-o. Let's clap Tony's name." *(Clap syllables with the class.)*

TEACHER NOW claps first Mary's name and then Tony's name. The class has to guess which is which. Do this until you have clapped the names of all the children in the class.

YOU WILL FIND that you will have duplicates—for example, "Mary Weston" will sound like "Peter Kersten" and "Tony Semolino" will sound like "Mary Ellen Stevens."

HAVE EACH child clap his or her own name. See if the children can identify others with the same name rhythms as their own.

BEAT OUT the rhythms with other parts of the body. Blink eyes, stamp feet, shake hips, move elbows. Use rhythm instruments to beat out the name rhythms.

A RHYTHM GAME that you can play is to pick three different names and:

> Clap hands together to rhythm of first name.
> Pat thighs for rhythm of second name.
> Stamp feet for rhythm of third name.

KEEP DOING these over and over while saying the names as you do the rhythm. It's a lovely rhythmic experience.

POETRY IN RHYTHM

PURPOSE—*To develop rhythm through speech.*

SELECT A favorite poem or nursery rhyme. Three examples, each with a different rhyming pattern, are:

Baa, Baa, Black Sheep	4/4 time
Hickory Dickory Dock	6/8 time
To Market, to Market	3/4 time

TELL THE children you are going to play a rhythm game. You say the first line of the poem and they echo (copycat) you.

TEACHER—Baa, baa, black, sheep.
CHILDREN—Baa, baa, black, sheep.
TEACHER—Have you any wool?
CHILDREN—Have you any wool?

CONTINUE until the class has learned the poem, then go through the poem without the echo. Thus:

TEACHER—Baa, baa, black sheep,
              Have you any wool?

CHILDREN—Yes sir, yes sir,
              Three bags full.

AS YOU KNOW, this is an excellent method of teaching anything—but this exercise will certainly teach the poem.

NOW, REPEAT the poem, substituting rhythm sounds for the words. Thus:

> Baa, baa, black sheep,
> Have you any wool?
> Clap clap clap clap
> Clap clap clap
> and so on. . . .

VARIATIONS—Clap two lines and speak two lines
                    Clap two lines and stamp two lines.
                    Divide into groups; each group claps a line.
                    Clap two lines and click tongues two lines.

                    Stamp two lines and pat thighs two lines.

SEE WHAT other ideas the class can come up with.

RHYTHM SOUNDS

PURPOSE—*To develop auditory discrimination.*

HOW MANY different ways can you make your voice sound? Changing your voice quality or the rhythm of your words is an excellent exercise in sound awareness.

PICK A WORD that is fun to say. Ice cream, pizza, hamburgers or marshmallows might be the start of a good list. Now, try saying your word in the following ways:

Hold nose	Loud or soft	Pucker lips
Cup hands over mouth	Fast or slow	Gruff or sweet

TEACHER AND class practice saying the word all the different ways. Now, let a child pick a word and the manner in which to say it. The class guesses what the word is after the child has said it. Let everyone have a turn.

NOW, GRADUATE to short sentences:

I like school.
Today is Monday.
Let's play tag.

SAY EACH sentence in all the different ways and have the children take turns again.

PLAY A variation of the game "gossip." Tell the children the way you are going to say a word but don't tell the word. Sit in a circle with the children and whisper the word in the first child's ear. This child passes on the word and it goes on around the circle. See what comes out at the end of the circle!

THIS KIND of game is wonderful for developing listening skills.

WHAT DOES IT SAY?

Words & Music
Miss Jackie Weissman

I see a hor - sy what does it say? ___ What does it say? ___

What does it say? ___ I see a hor - sy, what does it say? ___

Tell me what does it say? La la la la.

La la la la. La la la la la la.

I see a cow
I see a rooster
I see a duck
I see a dog
I see a mommy
I see a baby
   Etc.

WHAT DOES IT SAY?

PURPOSE—*Awareness of sounds.*

PARENTS AND children often play this game. As they see animals or pictures of animals, one asks the other, "I see a doggy. What does it say?" Parents ask the question as often as the children do.

YOU CAN play this game in the classroom, too. Prepare pictures of various animals. Sing the song "I See a Horsey" and substitute the various animals while showing the pictures of them. (Don't leave out the horsey.) As you sing the name of the animal, hold up the picture and have the children make the appropriate sound.

YOU WILL find that the children will sing along with you as they make the sounds.

HOW MANY different ways are there to say hello? "Hi," "How are you?" "Top o' the mornin'," "Shalom," "Bonjour," "Aloha," etc. Now, ask the children who would like to have his or her name in the song. Sing the song using the child's name and let the child say hello in any of the listed ways. For example, "I see a Susie and what does she say?" Susie then says hello in the way she has chosen.

A VARIATION is to sing the song and, instead of saying hello, have the children move in the appropriate manner. Do not use only animals—you can sing about mommy, daddy, baby, a firefighter, etc. For example: "I see a firefighter and what does she say?" etc.

ECHO RHYTHMS

Words & Music
Miss Jackie Weissman

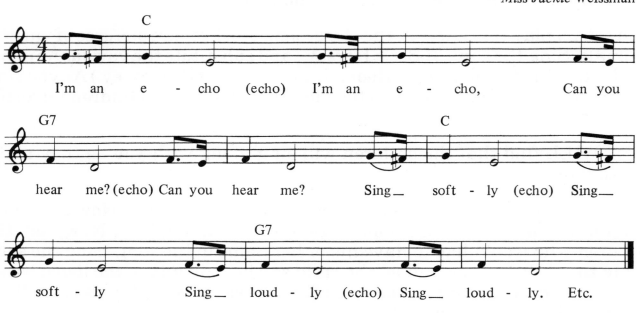

I'm an e - cho (echo) I'm an e - cho, Can you hear me? (echo) Can you hear me? Sing __ soft - ly (echo) Sing __ soft - ly Sing __ loud - ly (echo) Sing __ loud - ly. Etc.

Sing fast
Sing slowly
Sing high
Sing low
Sing happy
Sing sadly

    etc.

ECHO RHYTHMS

PURPOSE—*Listening and imitating sounds.*

ECHOES ARE reflections of sound that bounce back to you. Explain to the children about echoes. In the mountains, an echo bounces off the mountain back to you. In the classroom, an echo bounces back from teacher to the children and back.

THEY WILL understand the word "copycat." Say a word and have the children copycat you. This is an echo. Say the word in different ways—loud, soft, fast, slow.

NOW SING the song "Echo Sounds."

TEACHER—I'm an echo.
CHILDREN—I'm an echo.
TEACHER—Can you hear me?
CHILDREN—Can you hear me?
TEACHER—Sing softly.
CHILDREN—Sing softly.
TEACHER—Sing loudly.
CHILDREN—Sing loudly.

LET THE children play echo with each other. Echo all different kinds of sounds. Let the children make a sound and teacher echoes.

LONG VOWEL SONG

Words & Music
Miss Jackie Weissman

Hay Hay Hay. _____ Say Say Say. _____ The sound I like to hear is A.

Bay Bay Bay. _____ Day Day Day. _____ I like to hear the A.

Ho Ho Ho. _____ So So So. _____ The sound I like to hear is O.

Bo Bo Bo. _____ Do Do Do. _____ I like to hear the O.

Hi Hi Hi
He He He
Hu Hu Hu

LONG VOWEL SONG

PURPOSE—*Practicing saying long vowels.*

MANY CHILDREN need lots of practice in making various sounds, as they are still learning to talk. Singing is a happy way of practicing making sounds.

I HAVE USED four beginning sounds in "Long Vowel Song." If you have two- and three-year-old children, however, you may only want to use two beginning sounds. This is a very open-ended song and you can shape it to suit your needs.

SAY THE words with the children in a comfortable rhythm pattern. After they learn the words, you can sing it. Lots of repetition will help them learn, so sing the song many times.

HERE ARE a few ways you can use this song:

1. Make alphabet letters on big cards. Choose the letters that you are going to use in the song and let the children hold up the letters.

2. Assign specific sounds to specific children or groups. When it's time to sing that part of the song, this group can sing it.

3. Let the children or the groups decide what sounds they like, then have them find the sound in the alphabet pictures.

4. Use sounds that are the first letters of people's names, animals, things that are in the room or on the playground.

EENSY WEENSY SPIDER

Traditional

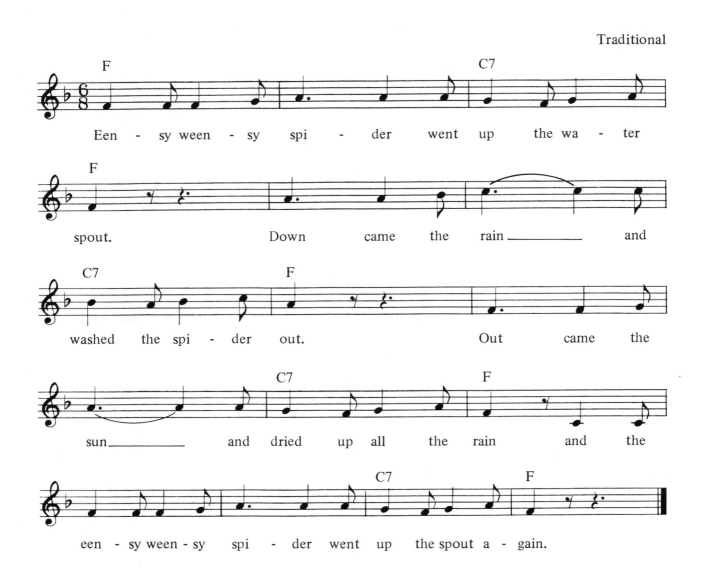

Een - sy ween - sy spi - der went up the wa - ter spout. Down came the rain _____ and washed the spi - der out. Out came the sun_____ and dried up all the rain and the een - sy ween - sy spi - der went up the spout a - gain.

EENSY WEENSY SPIDER

PURPOSE—*Developing beginning sounds.*

THIS GAME teaches many skills: listening, language and paying attention. First, learn the song; later, do the actions.

>Eensy weensy spider went up the water spout
>   *(Move fingers up to the sky like a spider)*
>
>Down came the rain and washed the spider out
>   *(Move hands down from the sky like rain)*
>
>Out came the sun and dried up all the rain
>   *(Make a big circle with hands for the sun)*
>
>And the eensy weensy spider went up the spout again
>   *(Move fingers up to the sky like a spider)*

AFTER THE children have learned the song, sing it many times in many different ways. The actions are the same, however, no matter how many different ways that you sing it.

SOME WAYS to sing "Eensy Weensy Spider":

>La la la
>Hum
>Whistle
>Beginning letter sounds—ga, ga, ga; da, da, da; ta, ta, ta
>Ooooooooooohhhh
>No singing, only the actions—you'll be amazed at how quiet the children are!

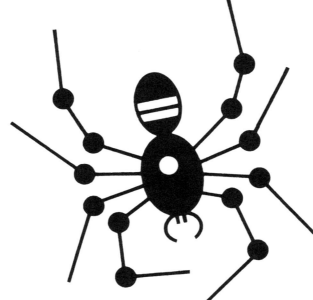

DIFFERENT LANGUAGES

PURPOSE—*Awareness of different languages.*

THE EXISTENCE of different languages throughout the world is one of the most fascinating facts of life. Where did all these languages come from? Why do they sound so different? Some are soft and rhythmic, some seem harsh and gutteral, some are sing-song and musical.

IF YOU HAVE a foreign-language-speaking child in the class, you are lucky: you can expose the other children to another language. Have this child teach the other children some common words, such as "cat" and "dog." What do these words sound like in the foreign language? Your children will love this, and there will be a lot of foreign words spoken at home tonight as the children show off their new knowledge.

TEACH THE children Pig Latin. If you don't know how to speak it, it's easy! Take the beginning sound of each word and put it at the end of the same word with the sound of a long *a*. For example: *mother* is "other-may," *father* is "ather-fay," *dog* is "og-day," *cat* is "at-cay."

CREATE YOUR own secret language for the class. Say all words with the same sound at the beginning, such as *d*: "I'm going to school" becomes "Dime doing do dool"; "Good morning, teacher," becomes "Dood dorning, deacher."

MAKE UP sounds that can stand for certain everyday words: stamp feet for "hello," beat chest for "goodbye," cough for "yes," click tongue for "no." During the day, instead of using "hello," "goodbye," "yes" and "no," the children will use the rhythms instead. Let some of the words be "secret," known only to the class.

YOU HAVE just taught the children a valuable lesson in language!

COGNITIVE SKILLS

CHILDREN LEARN through play. With rhythm experiences in play, a young child will begin to develop a sense of rhythm in his or her total self.

THE GAMES in this chapter are designed to develop cognitive thinking through experiences in rhythm.

RHYTHM SHAPES

PURPOSE—*Visualization of rhythm and sound patterns.*

LOOK AT the following shapes and try to make a sound that describes the shape. Use any syllable to make the sound—for example, "la."

The sound here might be "SEEEEEEEEE."

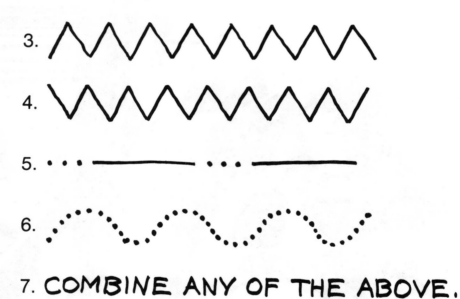

1. C C C C C

2. ▬▬▬▬ ▬ ▬▬▬ ▬

HERE ARE some other shapes:

3. ᴧᴧᴧᴧᴧᴧᴧᴧᴧᴧᴧ

4. ᴠᴠᴠᴠᴠᴠᴠᴠᴠ

5. ••• ▬▬▬ ▬▬▬ ••• ▬▬▬

6. (dotted wavy line)

7. **COMBINE ANY OF THE ABOVE.**

DRAW THESE shapes on large pieces of paper. Ask the children to describe the sound and/or rhythm pattern that each shape suggests. Or, give each child his or her own shape to describe.

THIS IS a very creative exercise. You will have many different answers for each shape. Remember, there are no wrong answers, only different versions of the "correct" answer.

Here's another variation: Have each child draw a shape on a piece of paper. The other children guess the sound or rhythm pattern.

ART RHYTHMS

PURPOSE—*To express rhythm patterns in art.*

CHILDREN LEARN through involvement. The greater the involvement, the greater the learning. Expressing rhythm patterns in art is not only a way to learn the concept of rhythm, it is a way to understand order, organization and discipline.

THE TEACHER draws various designs on large pieces of paper. Some examples are shown below.

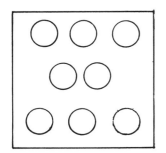 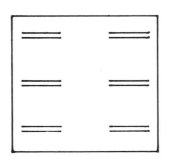 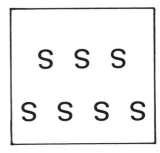

POINT OUT that the same pattern has been used over and over. Have the children choose one of your patterns, or let them have the option of creating one of their own. Either option is equally valid. Using large paper and crayons, the children create a rhythm picture. When the pictures are completed, have the class discuss each picture as to how the same pattern has been used over and over again.

ANOTHER WAY to create a rhythm pattern is to form patterns of patterns —thus:

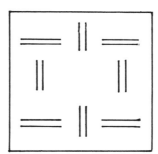

ANOTHER WAY to form patterns is to cut shapes from construction paper and paste them—in patterns—on large pieces of paper.

ALSO TRY using beans, corn, shells, etc. to paste shapes on paper. This is rhythm in another dimension, as you can feel the patterns with your fingers.

CREATE A RHYTHM

PURPOSE—*Developing awareness of rhythm patterns.*

BE A RHYTHM

TELL THE children that today they are going to be rhythms. They can be either "see" rhythms, "hear" rhythms or "feel" rhythms. For example:

SEE RHYTHMS—Patterns in the environment (see "Rhythm in the Room," page 34), clothes, wall, ceiling, floor.

HEAR RHYTHMS—Clock, windshield wiper, auto motor.

FEEL RHYTHMS—Heartbeat, pulse, cat purring.

TEACHER THEN asks each child in turn, "What rhythm are you?" The child answers, "I am a (see/feel/hear) rhythm." The child then acts out the rhythm while the class tries to guess what it is.

RHYTHM PICTURES

THE TEACHER prepares rhythm pictures. For example, a frog, clock, automobile, piano, washing machine, top, etc. Discuss with the class the rhythms suggested by each picture. Many objects can have several rhythms, such as a car or piano. Talk about whether the rhythm is fast or slow, smooth or bumpy.

PUT THE pictures face down. Choose one child to pick a card and then to make the rhythm suggested by the picture on the card. The other children try to guess what picture the child is imitating. Each child in class gets a turn.

THESE EXERCISES are not only rhythm lessons, they are wonderful in developing imagination and creativity.

LEARNING WITH RHYTHM

PURPOSE—*Learning the days of the week with rhythm.*

NAME THE days of the week by clapping your hands together while the children guess which day you are clapping. You'll soon see that all the days are the same except Saturday.

FIRST, CLAP ♩ ♩. The children will guess Monday, Tuesday, Wednesday, Thursday, Friday or Sunday. Then clap ♩ ♩ again. The children will again guess six different days. Then clap ♫ ♩ The children will correctly guess Saturday.

NOW, SAY the days of the week as the children clap the rhythm.

VARIATIONS—Say the days and clap Saturday.

Say the days in a soft voice and say Saturday in a loud voice.

Clap the days and stamp feet for Saturday.

Clap the days and say the word Saturday.

Stamp feet for the days and say the word Saturday.

HAVE THE children form a circle of seven children, each a different day. Starting with Monday, each child says his or her day in order. They say their days in a normal voice. When you get to Saturday, that child gets to yell "Saturday" in a BIG, outside voice.

KEEP CHANGING places until everyone has had a chance to be Saturday.

TALKING RHYTHM

PURPOSE—*To communicate through sound and rhythm.*

WHAT ARE some ways that you make sounds with your body?

> HANDS—Clap, slap, beat chest.
>
> FEET—Stamp.
>
> FINGERS—Snap.
>
> VOICE—Talk, sing, hum, moan, bark, howl.
>
> MOUTH—Blow, sigh, click, whistle.

DIVIDE THE class into several parts, with no more than six children to a "team." Each team chooses a musical body sound. Starting with Team One, teach them the following song: Clap, clap, clap, clap, clap, clap, clap (to the rhythm of "Mary Had a Little Lamb). Don't say "clap," just do it. Clap out the entire song until they have learned it. Then, go back and join the rest of the class. Have Team One clap out its song; the other children must guess what it is.

NOW, TAKE Team Two and teach them to stamp their feet to their song. (Use another familiar tune, such as "Yankee Doodle".) Continue until all the teams have had a chance.

IF TIME does not permit the entire class to participate, perhaps you can take one team per day (while the rest of the class is resting) and teach them their song.

TEACHING YOUNG children to communicate with their bodies is a good way to help them get in touch with themselves. This is also an excellent rhythm exercise.

FAST AND SLOW RHYTHMS

PURPOSE—*To understand fast and slow rhythms.*

FAST AND SLOW BODY MOVEMENTS

TEACHER SHOULD stand in front of the class where every child can see. Children do the movements along with the teacher. First, hold your arms straight out from your body. Make little circles with your hands—very slowly at first, then a little faster, faster still, then very fast.

DO THIS NOW with your fingers: bend them and straighten them, first very slowly, then a little faster, etc. Do various parts of the body—your head, shoulders, feet (sitting or lying on back) and so on.

FAST AND SLOW RHYTHMS

CHILDREN MOVE from one side of the room to the other. (This can be done outdoors—mark off boundaries.) Go from one side to the other in various ways—walking, running, hopping, skipping, jumping—slowly one way and fast on the way back. Pretend to be swimming, move like a cat, etc.

ANIMAL MOVEMENTS

THIS WOULD be an excellent exercise if you are going on a field trip to the zoo. Make a list of all the animals at the zoo and visit each one with the class. Which ones move fast? (Zebras, monkeys, birds.) Which ones move slowly? (Turtles, elephants, hippopotamuses.)

RHYTHM IN NATURE

PURPOSE—*To observe rhythm patterns in nature.*

PRACTICALLY everything in the world behaves according to its own rhythmic pattern. The seasons change, day changes into night, green leaves change to many colors, ocean and radio waves undulate according to certain frequences. Each of these things behaves with its own rhythm.

TAKE THE children for a rhythm outing. Tell them you are going to search for rhythm patterns in:

Leaf patterns	Icicle patterns
Flowers	Footprints in the snow
Anthills	Cloud patterns
Rock formations	Trees

EXPERIMENT with different kinds of movement on your rhythm walk. As the surface you are walking on changes, change your movement—hop on grass, tiptoe on concrete, stamp feet hard while walking across a baseball field, etc. Try varying your movement every half minute or so.

DEVELOP ART and dramatic activities from your rhythm walk. Have the children try to draw the various objects observed during the walk.

OBSERVING the world around us and its rhythms will help to develop young minds. A rhythm walk is not only fun, it's a very good lesson about the order found in the world.

CLASSIFYING SOUNDS

PURPOSE—*To develop listening skills.*

IN ADDITION to learning rhythm, children need to learn certain sound concepts. For example, children have difficulty with the concept of high and low. Understandably, they confuse it with loud and soft.

HERE ARE a few games that will help to establish the concept of high and low.

MOVE HIGH AND LOW

HAVE THE children use some fluttery object—preferably a scarf, but loose-leaf notebook paper will do. The fluttery movement of the object reinforces the location of the object as you play the game. Children hold the object high in the air—"high as the sky"—as they run from one side of the room to the other, then reach "low to the ground" as they continue to run from place to place. Explore other ways of moving, always with the fluttering object held high or low. Skip, gallop, hop, tiptoe, etc.

WALK TO THE SOUND

FIND TWO instruments, one that makes a high sound and one that makes a low sound. Pick two children, one for each sound, and have them stand behind the class. One child plays his or her instrument and the class has to guess whether this was the high or low sound. The first child to guess correctly gets to be one of the soundmakers. (You can use the voice as an instrument, too!)

WALK TO THE RHYTHM

A VARIATION of the game above: as the children play their sounds, have them play with a certain rhythm. Choose one of the children to walk to the rhythm while the class guesses the sound.

THE SCALE—SING HIGH AND LOW

SING A SCALE from low to high—do, re, mi, fa, so, la, ti, do. Begin with your hands on your toes (c'mon, you can do it!) and, as you sing the scale, gradually rise up until, on the final "do," you are on your tiptoes reaching for the sky. Then start high and gradually come down until your fingers are back on your toes. If you have an exercise time set aside every day, this would be an excellent time to play this game.

COGNITIVE GAMES

PURPOSE—*Developing awareness of rhythm.*

1. PLAY MUSIC on a phonograph. Have the children move to the rhythm of the music. First clap hands, then click tongues, stamp feet, and so on.

2. DRAW THE rhythm of the song on the blackboard. Slow rhythms will be soft, wavy lines; fast rhythms will be pointed. What would a march look like?

3. SHOW THE children how to make a clicking sound with their mouths. This will sound like a maraca. Half the class sings the song with the phonograph, the other half accompanies the singing with the maraca sound.

4. SING THE song "Old MacDonald." On the e-i-e-i-o part, make a rhythm sound. As above, clap hands, stamp feet, click tongues, etc.

5. SING THE song from Sesame Street—"One of These Things Is Not Like the Other." Tap out three rhythms on your table. Two of them can be 3/4 time, one can be 4/4 time. These times are played like this: using your left hand as number one and your right hand for number two, 1-2-2 is 3/4 time, 1-2-1-2 is 4/4 time.

MORE COGNITIVE GAMES

PURPOSE—*Ideas for developing rhythm awareness.*

1. WHAT IS your favorite song? Teach it to the children by singing it through several times until the children are sure of the words. Now, divide the song into two parts. Class sings the first part in a soft voice and the second part in a loud voice. Now, reverse the procedure—the first part in a loud voice and the second part in a soft voice.

2. PICK A child to hide behind something—a post, a door, a chair. Have the child make a sound. The class tries to guess what the sound is. Whoever guesses correctly gets to make the next sound.

3. MAKE SOUNDS with your body: stamp your feet, snap your fingers, click your tongue. Then, have one child make his or her body sound while the other children hide their eyes. The children guess what the sound is, and whoever guesses correctly is next.

4. REACH YOUR hands way up into the air "all the way to the sky." Then, reach down "into the valley." Tell the children that when you make a high sound they should imitate you and reach all the way to the sky. When you make a low sound they reach down low into the valley.

RHYTHM IN THE ROOM

PURPOSE—*Awareness of rhythm patterns in a room.*

THERE ARE many rhythms right in your classroom that you may not be aware of. This exercise will reinforce the definition of rhythm that has been stated earlier.

OBSERVE THE walls. Notice the rhythm of paneling, of window panes, of drapes or curtains.

LOOK AT the floor. Do you see rhythmic patterns in the linoleum, carpeting or wood floor? You can see a definite rhythm in the wood grain of a bare floor.

HOW ABOUT the ceiling? Does it have acoustical paneling? Light fixtures are usually symmetrical (rhythmic).

YOUR CLOTHES have rhythm. Look at the stripes, floral patterns, dots or checks on your garments.

ASK THE children to point out rhythmic patterns that they see in the room.

HAVE THREE children come to the front of the room. Observe rhythm patterns in their clothing. Ask the rest of the class to identify which child has the rhythm pattern that you announce.

THE TEACHER announces she sees a certain rhythm pattern in the room. The children look around until they find the pattern and then they run to wherever that pattern is perceived.

SING "I Can Feel the Rhythm" (p. 54) and change the words to fit your room: "I can see the rhythm of the floor" or "Johnny has a rhythm on his shirt."

HAVE AN art project. Tell the children to draw the rhythms in the room. Discuss the pictures with the class and find the rhythms suggested in the pictures.

BE A RHYTHM

PURPOSE—*Creating rhythm from pictures.*

THIS IDEA takes a little work, but it's well worth it. Use your—and the children's—natural creativity and you will have a very stimulating game.

PREPARE BADGES with pictures of rhythms on them. For example: rain, blowing leaves, child running. Paste pictures of rhythms or of things in nature that have a natural rhythm. Let the children select their own badges. Each child must make the rhythm suggested by his or her badge.

HERE ARE some ways the game can be played:

1. Whenever a child's name is called, he or she must answer with the rhythm.

2. Pick several of the children to make their rhythms. Make up a story using these rhythms.

3. Let the children pick a different rhythm badge each day.

4. Vary the speed with which the children make their rhythms—fast/slow, loud/soft, etc.

5. Let the children trade badges.

6. Have the children form a circle. On the count of three, each child passes his or her rhythm badge to the child at the left. Then, each child makes his or her new rhythm. You may want to point out to the children that there are many ways to do things and that they have choices.

CLAP A RHYTHM

PURPOSE—*Beginning rhythm reading.*

THIS GAME is very challenging to young minds. It is a wonderful way to begin music reading.

TEACHER MAKES some large charts (as illustrated below). There are two basic elements: a note and a rest.

       This is a note. ♩

       This is a rest. 𝄽

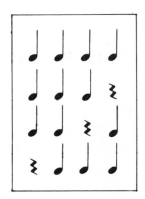 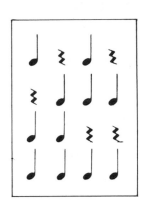 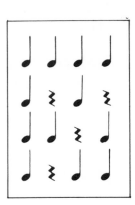

THE CHILDREN clap when teacher points to a note and hold their hands together when teacher points to a rest. Teacher goes slowly from left to right in a steady manner.

TRY TO CREATE a rhythmic feeling as you go through the rhythm patterns. You'll find that the children will do very well at this after only a short practice period.

AN ADDED BONUS: this is an excellent prereading experience.

MOVEMENT

CHILDREN RESPOND to music naturally. Moving rhythmically helps develop coordination and spatial concepts while encouraging creative movement.

AS YOUR BODY expresses rhythm, you internalize its nature and it becomes a part of your persona to be used at another time.

I BRUSH MY TEETH

Words & Music
Miss Jackie Weissman

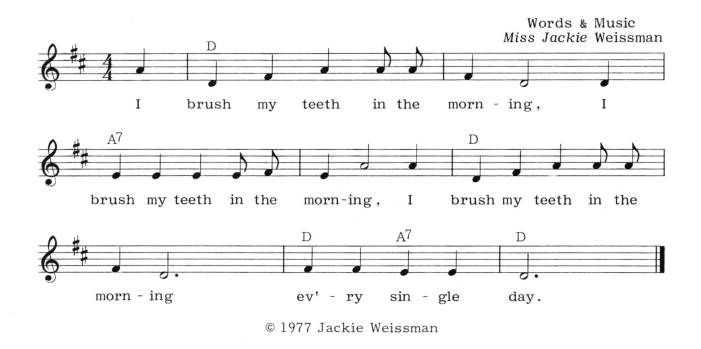

I brush my teeth in the morn - ing, I brush my teeth in the morn-ing, I brush my teeth in the morn - ing ev' - ry sin - gle day.

WITH each verse, first sing the song and then do the action.

I comb my hair

I wash my face

I wash my hands

I drink my milk

MAKE up more verses that are appropriate for you and the children.

I BRUSH MY TEETH

PURPOSE—*A rhythm action song used for recall.*

TEACH THE song "I Brush My Teeth" to the children. Teacher sings the song to the children, then the children sing along. Keep singing the song over and over (three or four times should be enough) until the children learn the song.

THE TEACHER starts a discussion about what everybody did when they woke up this morning. You will get lots of different answers—ate breakfast, got dressed, brushed my teeth, took a bath, etc. When a child says something that can be acted out, have the whole class do so—for example, for "combed my hair," each child pretends to hold a comb and then combs his or her own hair. You'll soon have plenty of actions to go along with this song.

NOW, DO the action as you sing the song: on "I brush my teeth in the morning," children hold their "toothbrush" to their mouths and pretend to brush their teeth. On "I comb my hair in the morning," they pretend to comb their hair.

EXTEND THIS idea to other activities. "I go to school in the morning" will lead to many of the things seen and done while walking to school or riding in the car or bus. "I went on a trip last summer" will recall many memories of last year's vacation.

RHYTHM IN THE WIND

PURPOSE—*Awareness of rhythms in nature.*

DISCUSS THE wind. What is the wind? What causes it? What causes the wind to change directions?

WHAT KINDS of things are blown about by the wind? (Leaves, kites, balloons, dust, etc.) Does a leaf blow slowly, fast, evenly, unevenly? How about snowflakes, raindrops, hail?

HAVE THE children pretend to:

> Be a leaf and flutter to the ground slowly.
> Be a leaf and blow across the yard quickly.
> Be a hailstone and fall to the ground.
> Be raindrops falling to earth.
> Be a feather and be blown by the wind.
> Be a snowflake and be blown by the wind.

DISCUSS WHICH of these blow with the same rhythm and which blow with different rhythms.

HOW DOES the wind feel? In the summer? In the winter? How does it feel if you are riding in the car with the window open? How does the rhythm of the wind feel?

WIND GAME

Each child chooses what kind of object he or she is and what kind of wind is blowing. For example, a balloon being blown by a gentle wind, a feather being blown by a strong wind.

BABY RHYTHM GAME

PURPOSE—*To experience a rhythm pattern.*

HERE IS a simple rhythm game that is lots of fun. Divide the class into four parts. Each group claps separately.

GROUP ONE—Clap four times—

GROUP TWO—Clap four times—

GROUP THREE—Clap four times—

GROUP FOUR—Shout, "Hey, baby," and shake arms in the air.

KEEP THE rhythm going on an even beat. As soon as group one claps its fourth beat, group two starts on its first beat. It may help to clap louder on the first beat of every four.

NOW, CHANGE the action: snap fingers, click tongues, stamp feet, jump up and down.

TRY CHANGING the rhythm pattern in the first three lines. Here are some alternate rhythms—

REMEMBER, THE last line is always the same: "Hey, baby."

I'M A WALKIN

Words & Music
Miss Jackie Weissman

I'm a walk - in' walk - in', walk - in', I'm a
walk - in', walk - in', walk - in', I'm a walk - in', walk - in',
walk - in', (Clap) Now I stop.

I'M A WALKING

PURPOSE—*Movement activities to develop motor skills.*

THESE ACTIVITIES will surely become some of the children's favorites. You can use them at recess, at lunchtime or at the end of the day as the children leave the room.

THE CHILDREN line up in single file or in pairs. As you sing the song, the class moves around the room in the manner suggested by the song. The clap is the signal to stop and freeze in place.

HERE ARE some ways to "walk" around the room:

> I'm a walking
> I'm a skipping
> I'm a hopping
> I'm a jumping
> I'm a skating
> I'm a swimming
> I'm a running

WHAT OTHER ways can you think of? Have the children make suggestions.

ALL THE FISH

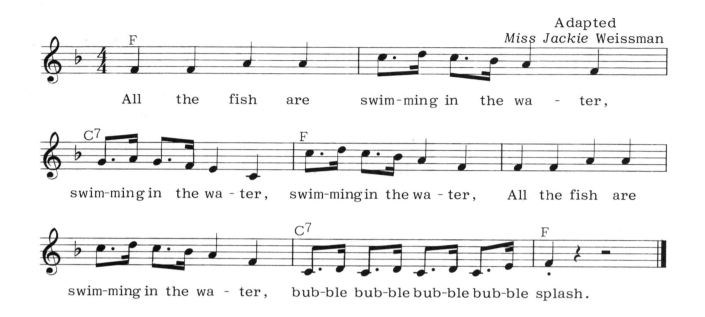

Adapted
Miss Jackie Weissman

All the fish are swim-ming in the wa - ter,

swim-ming in the wa - ter, swim-ming in the wa - ter, All the fish are

swim-ming in the wa - ter, bub-ble bub-ble bub-ble bub-ble splash.

THE feedback that I have gotten from parents over the years is that this song is an absolute favorite.

A MOTHER of six month old baby boy recently told me that she was diapering her baby and he was doing the actions of the fish song and trying to say "bubble bubble".

PUT YOUR hands together (palms flat touching each other) and move them around like fish swimming in the water. On the "splash" part, push them apart and pretend you are splashing someone.

A FUN way to sing the song is to get on the floor on your tummy.

MAKE UP new verses. "All the frogs are hopping in the water," "All the ducks are quacking in the water."

IF YOU are singing this in the bathtub, be prepared with towels!!

ALL THE FISH

PURPOSE—*To develop motor skills and have fun.*

THERE ARE a variety of activities that can accompany this song. First, teach the class the song.

1. THE CHILDREN sit in a circle facing one another, put their hands together (palms flat, touching each other) and move them around like fish swimming in the water as they sing the song. On the "bubble, bubble" part the children will naturally become louder and louder until *SPLASH!!* as they "splash" one another. A variation on this is to have the children get on their tummies and pretend to swim.

2. MAKE UP a new verse, for example, "All the ducks are quacking in the water." Have the children do a "duck walk" as they sing. Instead of "bubble, bubble" they "quack, quack."

TRY USING "All the frogs are hopping in the grass." The children hop like frogs and at the end say "ribbit, ribbit."

3. ANOTHER VERSE could be "All the birds are flying in the air." The children "fly" around the room and at the end say "cheep, cheep."

WHAT OTHER kinds of animal sounds can you think of?

TAP YOUR FEET

PURPOSE—*Expressing rhythm with body movement.*

THIS RHYTHM poem can be done by the whole class. The children will have to listen carefully to follow the instructions. Teacher is the leader.

Hello, feet *(tap ball of foot on the floor)*
Let's feel the beat.

Hello, knees *(bend knees)*
Zip a dee dee!

Hello, thigh *(move leg back and forth)*
My, oh, my.

Hello, hip *(roll hips round and round)*
Pip, pip, pip.

Hello, shoulder *(move shoulders in a circular motion)*
Get a little older.

Hello, neck *(stretch neck)*
Picky picky peck.

Hello, head *(turn head back and forth)*
Go to bed *(lay head on shoulder, close eyes and mouth, "sleep")*.

SOMETIMES the children like to snore!

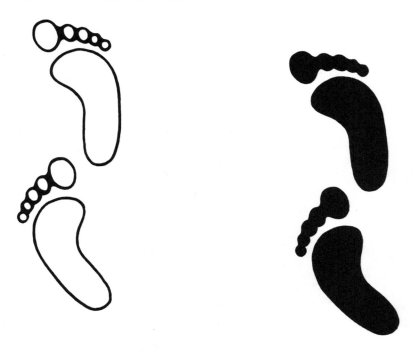

CLAP YOUR HANDS

PURPOSE—*To develop body control and social skills.*

TELL THE children they are going to learn to make rhythms with partners. Each partner has to cooperate with the other in order for this game to work.

BEFORE PAIRING off, teacher leads the class in a practice session using pretend partners. For the practice, teacher tells the children to pretend someone is sitting in front of them. The children pretend to talk to the person: "Hello, how are you?" "Want to play a clapping game?"

NOW, PRACTICE the clapping game:

> Clap hands on thighs two times.
> Clap hands together two times.
> Clap partner's hands two times (palms straight up).
> Clap your own hands two times.

PRACTICE THIS game several times. It may help to count the "one-two" as you clap each time. Practice clapping three times each time, then four times.

NOW, DIVIDE the class into pairs. Practice the part where they clap each other's hands, then play the whole game.

THIS IS an old Dutch game. You may have seen it in some old movies, performed in a comic manner by Laurel and Hardy, Abbott and Costello or Bing Crosby and Bob Hope. It's fun to play—and not as easy as it sounds.

TRY PLAYING the game while reciting the words to a song like "Yankee Doodle" or "Jingle Bells."

FOLLOW THE LEADER

PURPOSE—*To imitate rhythm patterns and to teach careful observation.*

TEACHER AND children sit in a large circle. Teacher, who is the leader, chooses a rhythm and the class imitates. Tap floor, tap knees, stamp feet, clap hands. The children must watch carefully because the leader can change the rhythm often.

VARIATIONS—The leader stands within the circle and does rhythm with the feet only—stamp, hop, jump, skate, etc. Children imitate the leader.

The leader does rhythm with various parts of the body—swing arms, shake hips, turn head, wiggle fingers. Children imitate the leader.

A child leaves the room. When he or she returns, the class is doing a rhythm pattern. The child has to guess who is leader. Everybody gets a turn at leaving the room and coming back and guessing.

SPEAK WITH YOUR BODY

PURPOSE—*To develop body control and imagination.*

CHILDREN CAN be very expressive with their bodies. This exercise is good to loosen up the body and is also a lot of fun. Tell the children they are going to learn to speak with their bodies.

HOW DO YOU say "yes" with your body? You shake your head up and down. How do you say "no"? You shake your head back and forth. Practice this a few times with the children.*

ALL THE PARTS of your body can say "yes" and "no." When you move up and down you say "yes"; when you move back and forth you say "no." Practice saying "yes" with your head, arms, shoulders and elbows, then say "no" with your head, arms, shoulders and elbows. Say "yes" with your hips, legs, ankles and toes, then say "no" with your hips, legs, ankles and toes.

MAKE UP questions that can be answered "yes" or "no." For example:

> Do you like pizza?
> Do you like ice cream?

TELL THE children that you are going to ask questions and that they are to answer with their bodies, NOT with their mouths. Then, give the children a turn. Tell them to ask a question that can be answered with "yes" or "no."

TRY HAVING a full day when the children are to speak "yes" or "no" with their bodies instead of their lips. You will find that the children pay very close attention all day.

* See the song "No, No, No" in *Sniggles, Squirrels and Chicken Pox,* a book by "Miss Jackie" Weissman.

I TAKE MY LITTLE HAND

Words & Music
Miss Jackie Weissman

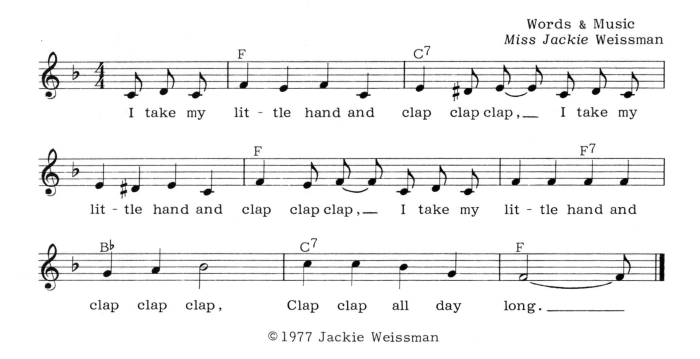

I take my lit - tle hand and clap clap clap,— I take my
lit - tle hand and clap clap clap,— I take my lit - tle hand and
clap clap clap, Clap clap all day long.—

2. I take my little hand and wave bye, bye, by. (3 ×)
   Bye, bye all day long.

MAKE UP other things to do with your hands. Shake, scratch, snap

3. Tap tap all day long.
   I take my little foot and go tap, tap, tap. (3 ×)

MAKE UP other things to do with your foot. Shake, hop, stamp.

TRY singing the song and making mouth sounds. This is excellent for language development.

I TAKE MY LITTLE HAND

PURPOSE—*Response to a rhythm pattern.*

CHILDREN LOVE to sing this song. It is open-ended, allowing for endless creative possibilities.

IT'S HELPFUL to tell children what is going to happen in a song before you sing it. This helps them to be ready when the time comes to do the action. Tell them that this song asks them to do certain actions with their hands.

SING THE song through and ask the class what the song told them to do. Sing it again with the children, doing the clap-clap-clap action.

NEXT, TELL them the song is going to tell them to wave bye-bye, then sing the song and do the bye-bye action. You might want to alternate on verses like this. One time, you can do the action and say the words at the same time; other times, you can do the action without saying the words.

VERSES FIVE and six can be used to build good self-image. Examples:

> I take my little mouth and say I'm a good _____ .
> I take my little mouth and say I'm so happy.
> I take my little mouth and say I feel good.

SUBSTITUTE other parts of the body. Examples:

> I take my little finger and shake, shake, shake.
> I take my little elbow and wave, wave, wave.
> I take my little feet and hop, hop, hop.

YOU CAN use this song with a class of any size. Children enjoy playing this game with a partner. On the clap-clap-clap part, the partners can clap each other's hands. They can also bump hips, slide together holding hands, etc.

THIS SONG'S open-endedness enables both teacher and child to vent their creative energy.

EVERYDAY RHYTHMS

PURPOSE—*To recognize rhythm patterns in everyday life.*

THERE IS rhythm all around us. Teaching children to observe the rhythm around them helps them to be aware of themselves and their environment.

DISCUSS WITH the children the different kinds of work that people do. (Avoid sex-role stereotypes when having a discussion such as this.)

TEACHER—What kind of work does your mommy do?
CHILD—Cooks, drives a bus, helps my dad clean the house.

TEACHER—What kind of work does your daddy do?
CHILD—Reads mail, washes dishes.

TEACHER—What kind of work do you do?
CHILD—Pick up toys, help parents.

HAVE THE class act out the work ideas the children give you. Try to have them act out the ideas in a rhythm pattern: "Hammer, hammer, hammer, hammer." "Pick up toys, pick up toys, pick up toys, pick up toys."

MAKE A RHYTHM GAME

One child is the "worker." Everyone says this poem:

> Work a rhythm
> Work a rhythm
> Work a rhythm now.
> Work a rhythm
> Work a rhythm
> I will show you how.

THE "WORKER" then acts out the work rhythm and the class tries to guess what the work is.

RHYTHM OF THE RAIN

PURPOSE—*Awareness of rhythms and sounds in nature.*

THIS IS a creative dramatic game that involves body movement. It is very effective in creating a mood. Once you teach it to the children, they'll ask to play it over and over again.

FIRST, SPEAK the words:

> Rain, rain, go away,
> Come again another day.
> Everybody wants to play.

SING THESE words using any two notes of the scale. Do the following actions and have the class follow you.

> Make soft raindrops *(snap fingers softly).*
> Make loud raindrops *(snap fingers loudly).*
> Make very loud raindrops *(slap hands on thighs).*
> Make thunder *(stamp feet).*
> Make lightning *(clap hands sharply).*

NOW, REVERSE the procedure until you have come back to the soft raindrops. Then, sing the song again.

I CAN FEEL THE RHYTHM

Words & Music
Miss Jackie Weissman

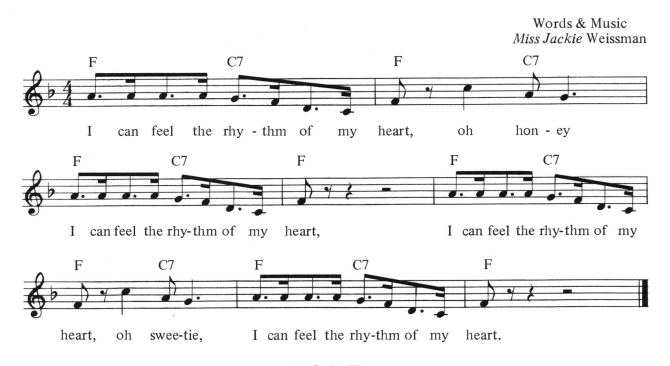

I can feel the rhy-thm of my heart, oh hon-ey
I can feel the rhy-thm of my heart, I can feel the rhy-thm of my
heart, oh swee-tie, I can feel the rhy-thm of my heart.

2. I can feel the rhythm of my pulse, oh sugar
   I can feel the rhythm of my pulse,
   I can feel the rhythm of my pulse, oh lovey
   I can feel the rhythm of my pulse.

3. I can feel the rhythm of my world, oh momma
   I can feel the rhythm of my world,
   I can feel the rhythm of myself, oh baby
   I can feel the rhythm of myself.

I CAN FEEL THE RHYTHM

PURPOSE—*To identify and develop a feeling for rhythm.*

WE ALL HAVE our very own individual rhythms within our bodies. Everybody's heart beats in a slightly different way.

SHOW THE children where their hearts are. Put hands on hearts and feel the steady, rhythmical beat. Ask the children, "Does your heart beat with a steady beat? Is your heartbeat smooth, hard, soft, tickly?" Explain that this is rhythm—a feeling that happens over and over again, the same way every time.

NOW, SWITCH to the pulse on the wrist. Show the children where their pulse is. Have them feel their own pulses and each other's pulses. Explain again that this is rhythm.

YOU CAN USE this as a simple lesson in physiology if you think it appropriate. The pulse and the heartbeat are, of course, both reflections of the heart's activity in pumping blood through the body, bringing oxygen and food to the cells.

SING "I Can Feel the Rhythm."

> I can feel the rhythm of my heart *(hands on heart)*
> Oh, honey *(wave arms vigorously in the air)*
> I can feel the rhythm of my heart *(hands on heart)*
> I can feel the rhythm of my pulse *(finger on pulse)*
> Oh, sweetie *(wave arms vigorously in the air)*
> I can feel the rhythm of my pulse *(finger on pulse)*

YOU CAN introduce variations on the "Oh, honey" and "Oh, sweetie" parts. Wave hips, ankles, feet, heads and change the words to the children's ideas—for example, "Oh, Sally" (using child's name), "Oh, sugar," "Oh, lovey," etc.

THIS SONG is very popular with children and they love to make up words to go into the song. (Sometimes they get silly and start using words with food names, like "Oh, banana," "Oh, macaroni," etc.)

MARY MACK

Words: Traditional
Music: *Miss Jackie* Weissman

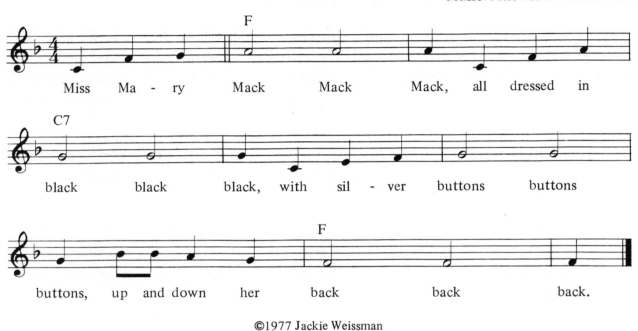

Miss Ma - ry Mack Mack Mack, all dressed in black black black, with sil - ver buttons buttons buttons, up and down her back back back.

2. She asked her mother, mother, mother
   For fifteen cents, cents, cents.
   To see the elephants, elephants, elephants
   Jump the fence, fence, fence.

3. They jumped so high, high, high
   They reached the sky, sky, sky
   And didn't come back, back, back
   Till the Fourth of Ju-ly, ly, ly.

MISS MARY MACK

PURPOSE—*Listening for a specific rhythm response.*

"MISS MARY MACK" is a traditional children's chant that has been set to music many times. The rhythm of the song seems to have a special appeal for children, and they will respond to the song both verbally and physically. Teach "Miss Mary Mack" to the children as follows:

1) Say the words slowly to the children.

2) Now, say the first line and let the children say the second line. Then, say the third line and have the children say the fourth line.

TEACHER—Miss Mary
CHILDREN—Mack, Mack, Mack
TEACHER—All dressed in
CHILDREN—Black, black, black . . .

3) Go through the entire song in this fashion.

4) Repeat the entire song, singing it this time.

5) Now the children know the song, so reverse the parts: the children sing the first line, teacher sings the second line, etc. Then, divide the class into two parts and let them trade lines while singing the song.

6) Now we begin to substitute sounds for words. For example:

Miss Mary
Clap   clap   clap
All dressed in
Clap   clap   clap

7) Use rhythm instruments for the clapping parts. Rhythm sticks, tone blocks or bells will work nicely. Explain to the children how they are going to use the rhythm instruments (hit on floor, shake, etc.).

8) Accompany each line with movement exercises. For example:

Miss Mary *(hands in air)*
Mack, Mack, Mack *(hands touch toes)*
All dressed in *(hands in air)*
Black, black, black *(hands touch toes)*

THE VARIATION possibilities are endless with this song. Let the children suggest some.

BUMP DITY BUMP

Words & Music
Miss Jackie Weissman

Take your fing - er and go like this bump di - ty bump di - ty

1. bump bump bump. 2. bump. Bump di - ty bump di - ty

bump bump bump. Bump di - ty bump di - ty bump bump bump.

Take your fing - er and go like this bump di - ty bump di - ty bump bump bump.

2. Take your hands
3. Take your shoulders
4. Take your arms
5. Take your hips
6. Take your legs
7. Take your toes

BUMP DITY BUMP

PURPOSE—*A rhythm response song.*

THE CHILDREN sit in a circle. Teacher tells them they are going to learn a new rhythm, "Bump Dity Bump."

THE TEACHER leads the class in saying "bump dity bump" over and over again. Keep saying the words without stopping and keep a steady rhythm going:

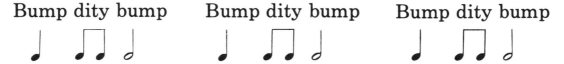

Bump dity bump   Bump dity bump   Bump dity bump

AFTER THE children have learned this rhythm, practice tapping on the floor while you say the words. Then practice tapping out the rhythm without saying the words.

NOW, ADD a new part to the rhythm. (Be sure to tell the children this is an addition to the regular rhythm.) Say "Bump dity bump dity bump bump bump." Accent the *bump* words—*bump* dity *bump* dity *bump bump bump.*

NOW, TEACH the children the song:

> Take your finger and go like this *(wiggle finger in the air)*
> Bump dity bump dity bump bump bump.
> Take your finger and go like this *(wiggle finger in the air)*
> Bump dity bump dity bump bump bump.
> Bump dity bump dity bump bump bump.
> Bump dity bump dity bump bump bump.
> Take your finger and go like this *(wiggle finger in the air)*
> Bump dity bump dity bump bump bump.

AFTER THE children have learned the song, it's time to tap out the rhythm without singing the song. Say "bump dity bump dity bump bump bump," first with your finger, now with your voice.

THIS IS a great song for loosening up the class and relieving tension. Try it just before lunch or recess.

VARIATIONS—It's fun to "bump dity bump" on different parts of your body—your head, your knees, etc.

Children also enjoy playing this game with a partner—where they can "bump dity bump" on each other.

I USE MY BRAIN

PURPOSE—*To identify body parts.*

THE USE OF large and small muscles helps coordination and develops a sense of rhythm and tempo. This will aid in the physical as well as the musical development of a child.

> I use my brain
> To think, think, think *(point finger at head).*
> I use my nose to smell *(sniff with nose while pointing at it).*
> I use my eyes
> To blink, blink, blink *(point finger at eyes and blink).*
> I use my throat to yell *(say "yell" in a loud voice, point finger at throat).*
> I use my mouth
> To giggle, giggle, giggle *(giggle and point at mouth).*
> I use my hips to bump *(bump against someone, point at hips).*
> I use my toes
> To wiggle, wiggle, wiggle *(wiggle toes and point at them).*
> I use my legs to jump *(big jump, point to legs).*

A VARIATION of this rhythm poem is to point to the part of the body and not say the name, only say what it does.

> I use my *(point to brain)*
> To think, think, think.
> I use my nose *(point to nose)* to smell.
> I use my eyes *(point to eyes)*
> To blink, blink, blink.
> I use my throat *(point to throat)* to yell.

Continue with the rest of the poem.

A SECOND variation of this rhythm poem is to clap the rhythm of the verbs. (You will notice that the rhythm is the same every other line.)

> I use my brain to *(clap clap clap).*
> I use my nose to *(clap).*
> I use my eyes to *(clap clap clap).*
> I use my throat to *(clap).*

Continue with the rest of the poem.

GET IN TOUCH WITH YOURSELF

PURPOSE—*To become aware of our body rhythm.*

BECOMING AWARE of our bodies is the first step in becoming aware of our total environment. This is a rhythm exercise that transfers the same movement to all parts of our bodies and makes us totally aware of our bodies.

THE TEACHER tells the children that they are going to practice waving. Everyone waves their hands in the air for half a minute or so; this will loosen up the class and the children will be ready to participate.

FIRST, PRETEND you are leaving home for school. Wave goodbye to your family.

WAVE—Fast
      Slowly
      To get somebody's attention (vigorously)
      To somebody you don't want to see (slowly, unenthusiastically)
      Happily
      Sadly
      With other parts of the body—Feet
                                  Elbow
                                    Hips
                                    Fingers
                                    Toes
  Fast—with your feet, elbows, hips, fingers and toes

A DRAMA GAME

PURPOSE—*Awareness of self through movement.*

MUSIC IS movement through sound. Rhythm is a steady movement pattern that happens over and over again. Children speak naturally with their bodies. This activity provides many opportunities for creative movement.

HERE ARE some ideas to get you started. Ask the children for their suggestions—they'll have many.

Part of the Body	What it Says
Nose	"I smell something yummy."
Nose	"I smell something yucky."
Eyes	"I'm happy."
Eyes	"I'm sad."
Eyes	"I don't understand."
Head	"Yes."
Head	"No."
Shoulders	"I don't know."
Hands	"Stop."
Foot	"I'm waiting."
Elbow	"Get away."
Neck	"I can't see."
Hands	"I like you."

AFTER THE class has done this activity long enough to understand what is called for, teach the following game.

THE CLASS sits in a circle. Teacher makes a statement with his or her body, for example, "Gee, am I tired." Children imitate the statement with their bodies. Next, the teacher's body might say, "I'm so happy," and children imitate. Now, go around the circle. Each child gets to make a body statement, with the whole class imitating.

SOUND OFF!

PURPOSE—*Expressing yourself through the medium of sound.*

HERE ARE some ways to make sounds:

Singing	Talking	Humming
Whistling	Breathing	Laughing
Hissing	Sighing	Sneezing
Coughing	Clapping	Clicking
Crying	Knocking	Slapping
Stamping	Tapping	Playing an instrument

CAN YOU think of any more?

THIS IS a game that asks you to make your body move the way the sound feels. Laughing and singing would indicate that you feel happy, and you move accordingly. Crying means you are sad, and you move as if you are sad. Coughing and sneezing mean you're sick, and so on. Help the children with suggestions at first.

YOU CAN make up a story using the various sounds above. Each time the children hear the sound, they move accordingly.

MUSIC SUGGESTS moods that can, in turn, suggest sounds. Play happy and sad music and have the children move according to their interpretation of the music.

SOME MOVING ideas are crawling, skipping with a smile, walking slowly, tiptoeing, elephant walking, etc.

WAVE SLOWLY with your feet, elbows, hips, fingers and toes.

NOW, COMBINE waving different parts of the body in different ways—wave happily with your elbows, wave sadly with your fingers, wave with your hands and your hips at the same time, wave with your foot (stand on the other foot) and your elbows at the same time.

WINTER RHYTHMS

PURPOSE—*Developing awareness of rhythm in nature.*

THERE ARE rhythm patterns in all of nature—the changing of the seasons, the regular occurrence of night and day, the hum of crickets, ocean waves, and on and on. There is also rhythm in snowfall.

SNOW HAS been a recurring theme in art. Frederick Chopin composed music about snow. Ralph Waldo Emerson, Robert Frost and many other poets have created poetry using snow as a theme. One also thinks of the wonderful winter scenes painted by Grandma Moses and others.

NOW IS A good time to discuss snow with the children. Can you hear the snow falling? Can you feel snow? How does snow feel when it falls on you— soft? cold? tickly? Does the snow fall straight down? Does it twirl around as it falls?

CREATE SNOW by tearing white paper into very small pieces. Get up very high and drop the "snow." Observe how it falls. Continue the discussion with the children as you do this several times. (You'd better organize a "snow removal crew," because you'll have lots of paper on the floor.)

HAVE THE children become snowflakes. They whirl, twirl and fall softly to the ground. What else falls softly like snow? Feathers, leaves, etc.

ACT OUT the following poem:

> Snowflakes, snowflakes,
> Whirling, twirling
> Snowflakes, snowflakes all around.
> Snowflakes, snowflakes,
> Whirling, twirling,
> Falling softly to the ground.

RHYTHM VARIATIONS

PURPOSE—*To involve the total self in rhythm.*

TEACHER MAKES a circle on the floor using masking tape or chalk. (Make the circle big enough for six children to walk around it without becoming dizzy.)

ASSEMBLE THE class in groups of six. Each group has its own circle. Teacher leads each group in walking around its circle. Teacher says, "Rhythm is something that happens over and over again."

TEACHER SAYS, "Sometimes rhythm can go faster." Each group walks faster around its circle. Teacher then says, "Sometimes rhythm can go slower." Each group walks slower. Teacher continues to give instructions about how to walk around the circles.

HERE ARE some ways to walk around the circles:

> BUMPY—jump on both feet around the circle.
> SMOOTH—glide feet as if skating.
> STRAIGHT—walk with feet directly in front of one another.
> SOFT—walk on tiptoe.
> FAST—walk very fast.
> SLOW—walk very slowly.
> STRONG—march with stamping feet.
> ZIG-ZAGGY—zig-zag around the circle.

CHILDREN ENJOY this kind of activity. Try other kinds of shapes—squares, triangles, rectangles. Play different kinds of music to inspire movement—marches, polkas, folk, country, jazz.

MIRROR SHADOW

PURPOSE—*To develop self-awareness and imagination.*

THIS GAME is quite popular. It's creative, open-ended and develops the imagination.

THE FIRST part of the game is called "Mirror." Each child has a partner. One child faces the partner and pretends to be looking into a mirror. The mirror imitates all of the actions of the person looking into it—if the person jumps up and down, the mirror jumps up and down; if the person turns around, the mirror turns around, too. Teacher may give suggestions as to various movements: shake hands, nod head, wave arms up and down, etc.

TRY THIS game with music. Let the children move to the music as the "mirror" imitates the movements.

THE COUNTERPART of this game is called "Shadow." It is played the same way, except that the shadow will follow the partner as they move around the room hopping, skipping, etc. Animal movements are very popular in "Shadow" and the children will have lots of fun making up these animal movements.

NOTICE: WHEN using music with this game, you will get lots of large movements and lots of noise if you play loud, marching music. If you play soft, gentle music, you will get slow and soft movements.

"MIRROR SHADOW" promotes one-to-one relationships, creativity of movement, exercise, body awareness and, most important, lots of fun.

RHYTHM DEVELOPS LISTENING SKILLS

I HAVE ALWAYS had the belief that if people would learn to listen to one another the world would be more peaceful.

ONE OF THE most important reasons for developing listening skills in young children is that you are also developing reading skills that will aid the child when he or she is ready to read. Listening skills are a very important prerequisite to reading.

AWARENESS OF SOUNDS

PURPOSE—*To become aware of sounds in the environment.*

IF WE LEARN to listen to all the wonderful sounds in the environment it will enrich our lives. However, we must be taught to listen. Here are some of the sounds we hear in our everyday environment:

    Wind   Fire engine   Dogs barking   Alarm clocks
    Doors slamming   Automobile horns   Train whistles

What others can you think of?

HAVE THE children imitate these sounds, one at a time. One child makes the sound, the other child guesses what it is.

WHAT KINDS of sounds do you make to your friends?

Knock on the door   Call on the telephone   Whistle   Tap on the window

HOW CAN you communicate by sound only? How do you say "I like you"? (Hug) How do you say "I'm angry"? (Stamp feet) How do you say "I'm tired"? (Yawn) How do you say "I'm hungry"? (Rub tummy)

WHAT ARE some other sounds in your environment?

SOUND OR SILENCE

PURPOSE—*To develop listening skills.*

DISTINGUISHING between sound and silence seems like an idea that doesn't have to be taught. It is, however, an important concept. In music, for example, the rests (silence) are just as important as the notes (sound). The following game is an enjoyable way to illustrate the difference between sound and silence.

TEACHER PLAYS a record on the phonograph. While the music is playing, the children should tiptoe around the room. When the music (unexpectedly) stops, the children freeze in place. Teacher will have to demonstrate what it means to freeze the first time. The children will learn very quickly and this will be the fun part of the game.

EVERYBODY SHOULD be very quiet in order to hear the music. You may want to play the phonograph very low so that everyone must be *very* quiet. Remember, sound means tiptoe and silence means freeze.

PLAY ANY kind of instrumental music you have available. Be sure it is instrumental music—vocal music may be distracting.

A VARIATION is to let one of the children make the music by singing or playing a rhythm instrument. When the child stops the music, the rest of the class freezes.

THIS IS a good game to set up sound control in your room. Explain to the children that whenever you say "freeze" all activity and sound in the room must come to a halt. Once you have taught this to the class, you'll have a very effective way to get the students' attention whenever they are getting restless.

THE CONDUCTOR GAME

PURPOSE—*To listen and follow rhythm directions.*

THE CONDUCTOR of an orchestra is the "boss." The conductor controls how fast or slow the music is played, how loud or soft the music is and, most important, the conductor controls THE BEAT. The players must watch the conductor at all times so that they can play the music the right way.

SOME CONDUCTORS use a baton—a thin stick—and other just use their hands. Children love to play at being a conductor, because then they can be the "boss." (Be sure everybody gets a turn.)

CONDUCTOR—I am the conductor
        Of a great big band.
        You can play the music
        If you watch my hand.

THE POEM ABOVE is about the "music" that's going to be played. Select a child to be the conductor. Let the conductor use a "baton" (a ruler, a pencil, a rhythm stick) if he or she wishes. The "orchestra" (class) says the poem according to the conductor's directions. The children can also pretend to be playing instruments while they say the poem. The conductor directs this way:

LOUD MUSIC—both hands in front of face, palms facing mouth. (For even louder music, make a "come on" motion.)

SOFT MUSIC—fingers to mouth in a "shhhh" motion.

MOVE BATON up and down to keep the beat—fast for fast music, slowly for slow music.

A FUN VARIATION is to play instrumental music on a phonograph or a tape recorder. Let the whole class be conductors as they react to the recorded music. Or, let them all be band members playing the music. (Make sure that they know what instrument they're playing and how it sounds.)

FEEL THE VIBES

PURPOSE—*Experiences with vibration.*

SOUND IS produced by movement of the air. This movement that is associated with sound is called "vibration." Here are some ways to experience vibration:

1. TOUCH YOUR hand to your throat. Now, hum. Can you feel your throat's vibration?

2. HOLD THE palm of one hand about an inch in front of your mouth. Now, blow on your hand. You will hear a faint but distinct sound. Take the index finger of your other hand and move it through the air flow. Hear the sound change?

3. CUT A rubber band so that it lies in one straight, flat piece. Two people hold the ends of the rubber band and stretch it out until it is fairly taut. A third person plucks the rubber band in the middle to produce a sound. Pull the rubber band tighter. The sound grows higher. (CAREFUL! Don't pull the rubber band too tight—it may snap and hurt someone.) Now, gradually loosen the rubber band while continuing to pluck. Notice the sound gets lower and lower as the rubber band is loosened.

4. THERE MAY be other things in the room that vibrate. Touch them, if possible, and try to imitate the sound they make. If you have an air conditioner, it will vibrate when turned on. Other appliances in the building that vibrate are electric typewriters, refrigerators and furnaces.

5. HERE IS an action poem about vibration. Put your hands over your head and shake your body as you say "vibraaaaaation."

> Vibraaaaaation.
> Everywhere vibraaaaaation.
> Going up sounds *(stretch arms up to the sky).*
> Going down sounds *(move arms down to the floor).*
> Vibraaaaaation, vibraaaaaation.
> Everywhere vibraaaaaation.

MATCH THE TONES

PURPOSE—*To improve the ability to match tones.*

YOUNG CHILDREN should learn to recognize differences in sound quality in order to pave the way for clarity of speech and listening ability.

TEACHER PUTS three objects on the table: a block, a book and a ball. It's a good idea to use three objects that start with the same sound.

THREE CHILDREN come to the table and pick up one of the objects. Teacher then asks, "Where is the block?" The child with the block holds it up. Teacher then asks, "Where is the ball?" The child with the ball holds it up. Teacher then says, "Where is the book?" and the book-holding child holds it up. Practice this a few times. The game then begins.

TEACHER ASKS the questions in different tones and the child answers in the same tone as the teacher. Here are some different ways to ask the questions:

Loud voice	Whisper	Hold your nose
Soft voice	Gruff voice	Fast
Sweet voice	Slowly	Loud and soft

LET THE children think of other ways to change their voices.

VARIATIONS—The children sing the questions and teacher answers.

One child asks the question, another child answers.

Sing the question. (Sing all the words in the same tone—it's too hard to try to match a melody AND match the voice quality.)

YOU CAN play a simple version of this game with an infant. Sing a sound to the infant four times—"Da da da da." Do this over and over and soon the infant will imitate you. After the baby learns this game, he or she will initiate the sound, and you should imitate the baby.

THE VOLUME GAME

PURPOSE—*To understand how music gets gradually softer and louder.*

HERE IS a game you can play with children to help them understand the concept of loud and soft. If you don't believe that this concept needs to be learned, just think of how many times you've had to say to a child, "Lower your voice."

CHOOSE A word that is fun to say. Repeat the word over and over. Start very softly and gradually get louder and louder. Have the children listen to you first and then have them say the word with you. Here are some fun words:

Ice cream	Picalilli	Spaghetti
Macaroni	Itsy-bitsy	Topsy-turvy

TEACHER AND the class say the word, starting softly with arms at your sides. As you get louder and louder, gradually raise your arms up to the sky. Then reverse: start loudly with hands over your head and gradually get softer as you lower your arms.

TRY SINGING the word as you do a simple exercise like the one above. Use one or two notes only so the exercise doesn't get too complicated.

THIS IS a good game for a learning center. After the children know the game they can do it alone or with others. They can also make a tape of themselves saying the words louder and softer and they can do the exercises to accompany their own voices.

THE LOUD AND SOFT GAME

PURPOSE—*To learn the concept of loud and soft.*

TRY TO FIND a recording of Haydn's "Surprise Symphony." It's worth the trouble, because children love this game. (If you can't find a recording, use the poem. It will still be effective.)

TELL THE children this story:

"Once upon a time there was a man named Mr. Haydn. He worked very hard at his job. His job was making up beautiful music for musicians to play on their instruments. One day Papa Haydn worked especially hard at his job and, when he came home, he fell fast asleep in his chair. When the children came into the room they thought he was playing a trick—so, at first, they were very quiet, and then, all of a sudden, they made a BIG NOISE and woke Papa Haydn up. He thought that it was a funny joke and so he wrote some music about it.

NOW, PLAY the second movement of the "Surprise Symphony." You will know when the surprise comes. You can use the following poem either with the music or by itself.

> Papa Haydn's gone to sleep *(children pretend to sleep).*
> Told the children, "Don't make a peep" *(children pretend they are*
>   *Papa Haydn, pointing their finger at the children).*
> But they were such naughty boys *(naughty facial expression),*
> Came and made a LOT OF NOISE *(VERY loud).*

SAY THE poem in a whispery voice until you come to the "lot of noise" part, then use a GREAT BIG VOICE.

ASK THE children if the music reminds them of any other song (the melody is very much like "Baa, Baa, Black Sheep," "ABC" and "Twinkle, Twinkle, Little Star").

I HEAR THE RHYTHM

PURPOSE—*Listening for rhythm words.*

THIS IS an exercise in listening for words within a poem or song. Tell the children that when they hear the rhythm word they are to wave their hands in the air. For example, in "Humpty Dumpty," have the children wave their hands in the air every time they hear "Humpty."

PICK SONGS and poems in which the same word appears more than once, such as "Pat-a-Cake," "This Little Pig," "Mary Had a Little Lamb," etc.

LET THE class think of other ways to signal. Jump up and down, wave hands, wiggle fingers, shake heads. Now reverse—the children sing the song and teacher makes the signal.

VARIATIONS—Select words that start with the same sound.

Pick a word that rhymes with a certain word.

Choose words that have the same ending sound.

AFTER YOUR class learns this game, try some sophisticated versions. You sing the song or say the poem and they make the signal when you say a word relating to a certain subject—for example, a color, number, animal, etc. This is especially good for children five and six years old.

YOU CAN play this game with recordings, too.

BANKS OF THE OHIO

PURPOSE—*To listen to—and sing back—a melody.*

THIS IS an exercise in echoing back a line of poetry or music. The teacher says the first line of the poem and holds the last word while the children echo back the entire line.

TEACHER—I asked my friend
CHILDREN—I asked my friend

TEACHER—To take a walk
CHILDREN—To take a walk

TEACHER—Just a little walk
CHILDREN—Just a little walk

TEACHER—Down beside
CHILDREN—Down beside

TEACHER—Where the waters flow
CHILDREN—Where the waters flow

TEACHER—Down by the banks
CHILDREN—Down by the banks

TEACHER—Of the O-hi-o.
CHILDREN—Of the O-hi-o.

SUBSTITUTE other words for "walk," such as run, skip, hop, jump. Have the children suggest other substitute words.

LET'S TAKE A WALK

PURPOSE—*To observe sounds around us.*

THERE ARE thousands of sounds that we hear every day. Many of these sounds are faint and indistinct; often we do not even notice them. It is a good exercise, however, to "get in touch" with the world now and then by doing some careful listening.

TAKE A WALK outdoors with the class on a nice, sunny day. Tell the children you are going to listen for various sounds. Here are some you might listen for:

Animal conversations	Bird conversations
Wind blowing	People talking
Dogs barking	Air conditioners humming
Birds chirping	Bees (and other insects) buzzing
Cars driving by	Lawn mowers

TAKE ONE sound at a time and tell the children to listen for it. When they hear the sound, they raise one hand. Do not go to the next sound until all the children have heard the assigned sound.

GET DOWN on the grass and listen to the earth. You will hear earth sounds and all of the sounds listed above in a different way.

WALK ON different surfaces. Take off your shoes and walk barefoot. Notice the different sounds your feet make with shoes and without shoes, on the sidewalk and on the grass.

FOLLOW UP on the walk with an art project. Have each child try to draw one of the sounds you observed on the walk.

MARVIN, MALCOLM AND MALVINA

PURPOSE—*To develop listening skills.*

THIS STORY contains words that must be listened for and acted upon. Tell the children to listen for the words "spinach," "dog" and "cat." When they hear the word, they make the appropriate sound. On the word "spinach," they say "yum, yum." On the word "dog," they bark like dogs. On the word "cat," they meow like cats.

THE TEACHER tells the story:

Once upon a time there was a little boy named Marvin who did not like the taste of *spinach*. Every time Marvin was served *spinach* for dinner, he would say, "*Spinach*, yuk."

Marvin's *dog* Malcolm loved *spinach*. Marvin's *cat* Malvina loved *spinach*. Everybody loved *spinach* but Malcolm. If Marvin did not eat his *spinach*, Malvina the *cat* and Malcolm the *dog* would fight over the *spinach*. The *dog* and *cat* made so much noise fighting over the *spinach* that all the neighbors began to say, "If you don't stop that noise, Marvin, you and your *dog* and *cat* will have to move away from here."

Marvin loved his little house and he surely did not want to move away. Malcolm the *dog* loved his house and he didn't want to move away. And Malvina the *cat* loved her little house and she did not want to move away.

WHAT COULD THEY DO????????????

LET THE children tell you the answer to the problem of Marvin, Malcolm and Malvina. They'll have a lot of fun and you'll get lots of different answers.

THIS IS a popular game. The children will never tire of it! You may want to try variations, such as using rhythm instruments—sticks, bells and maracas. When you say "spinach," the children with rhythm sticks hit their sticks on the floor. When you say "dog," the children with bells ring them. When you say "cat," the children with maracas shake them.

WHAT DO YOU HEAR?

PURPOSE—*To develop listening skills.*

HERE ARE some exercises that teach children to listen carefully and develop a feeling for where tones are placed.

1. FILL CONTAINERS—tin boxes, film cans, anything that cannot be seen into—that will transmit sound with various soundmakers (such as marbles, sand, sticks of wood, rubber balls and other objects which have distinctive sounds.) There should be two of each kind of soundmaker. Put the soundmakers into the boxes and let each child choose one. The game is for the children to match their sounds to one another. Then, have the children arrange themselves in a line according to the softest sound, then the next softest, etc., until you get to the loudest sound.

THE CHILDREN turn their backs. Put three objects on a table—for example, a glass, a milk carton and a tin box. Next, tap the objects, one at a time. The children have to identify the objects from the sound.

2. TEACHER SINGS "hello" in two tones, "hel-lo." The children try to sing back in the same two tones. Teacher then sings "Hel-lo John-ny," and the children try to match the tones again.

ALL OF THE above games are appropriate for a learning center and are activities that children can do with their peers.

TAPE RECORDER GAMES

PURPOSE—*To teach listening, organization and recall.*

THESE ARE some games you can play using a tape recorder.

GUESS THE SOUND

Prerecord four or five common objects—doors slamming, clock ticking, air conditioner humming, etc. Play each sound for the class and have them guess the object.

WHAT KIND OF SOUND IS IT?

Tell the children to identify the sound that slams (door), ticks (clock), hums (air conditioner).

WHERE DO YOU HEAR THE SOUND?

Record more sounds—doorbell, typewriter, drum—in addition to the sounds above. Play these and ask, "Where do you hear this sound? Who makes this sound?"

Play the sounds again. Describe each sound: what makes it, who makes it, what kind it is.

See if the children can remember the order in which the sounds were played.

SOUND STORY

Tape groups of sounds—school sounds, home sounds, outside sounds. Listen to the sounds and have the children identify them. Make up a story to go with the sounds.

TOM-TOM BEATS

PURPOSE—*To recognize a pre-set rhythm pattern.*

LONG BEFORE telephones, radio and television, people were able to communicate over long distances by other means. One of those means was the use of a loud drum that could be heard in the next village. One village could warn the other about danger or weather conditions, or notify the other about special events.

THIS GAME involves making conversation using drum beats. You can use any rhythm instrument for your drum, tapping on the table or floor.

START WITH a question and an answer—for example: "Hello, how are you?" "I'm fine, thank you." Create a rhythm for each of the above. (Do not use the rhythm of the words.)

SENTENCE	RHYTHM
How are you?	♩ ♩ ♫ ♩ ♫ ❘ ♩ ♩ ♩ 𝅗𝅥
I am fine, thank you.	♫ ♩ ♫ ♩ ♩ ❘ ♫ ♩ ♫ ♩ ♩

TEACHER ASKS the question by beating out the rhythm as above. The children answer using the answer rhythm. Practice this a few times until the children can do it, then add to the conversation.

SENTENCE	RHYTHM
How are you?	♩ ♩ ♫ ♩ ♩ ♫ ❘ ♩ ♩ ♩ 𝅗𝅥
I am fine, thank you.	♫ ♫ ♩ ♩ ❘ ♫ ♩ ♫ ♩ ♩
What is your name?	♩. ♪ ♩. ♪ ❘ ♩ ♩ 𝅗𝅥
My name is _____	♩ ♩ ♫ ♩ ❘ ♩ ♩ ♫ ♩

HAVE THE children talk to one another in this new language.

THIS IS a wonderful exercise in remembering and listening. One teacher who uses this game starts every morning with a rhythm that has been pre-decided to mean "Good morning." She does this with three different children each day; each child picks one of several predecided answers. Then, the rest of the class has to identify the answer.

LISTEN FOR THE RHYTHM

PURPOSE—*Awareness of rhythms in sound.*

CHILDREN ENJOY imitating sounds. How often have you heard them imitate train whistles, police sirens or airplane engines when they're playing with these toys? Many of these sounds have rhythm patterns that can be easily identified and imitated.

LISTEN TO some sounds with your class, such as:

Clock ticking   Windshield wipers   Water dripping   Metronome

LISTEN TO these sounds and list some more of your own. Discuss them with the class and try imitating them. Make the sounds in a definite and steady rhythm pattern. You can change the speed of the rhythm, but only gradually. Keep the rhythm as steady as possible.

RHYTHM SOUND GAME

AFTER THE whole class has listened to and imitated the sounds chosen in the exercise above, let individual children choose one sound to make for the class. The class has to guess what is the object making the sound. Be sure each child gets a turn. You may have to repeat sounds more than once, but the important thing is that each child gets to express himself or herself rhythmically.

RHYTHM SOUND SONG

THE SONG on page 54 can be used with substitute words. For example: "I can hear the rhythm of the water, oh honey," or "I can hear the rhythm of the wipers, oh honey." See if the children can make up some more verses.

RHYTHM SOUND WALK

TAKE A WALK around the school and the yard with a tape recorder. Find sounds that have a rhythmic pattern—a furnace, clocks, air conditioners, birds chirping, insects buzzing, etc. Play the recording for the students and let them try to identify the sounds.

I'VE GOT A RHYTHM

Words & Music
Miss Jackie Weissman

Leader: I've got a rhy - thm, lis - ten to my rhy - thm

I've got a rhy - thm, can you do it too.

*Leader claps four times,
stamps four times,
makes up own rhythms.*

Children imitate leader. This is my rhy - thm, you can do it too.

©1977 Jackie Weissman

I'VE GOT A RHYTHM

PURPOSE—*To imitate rhythm patterns.*

TEACHER SINGS,

> I've got a rhythm,
> Listen to my rhythm.
> I've got a rhythm,
> Can you do it too?

TELL THE children you are going to play a copycat game—you do the actions and they copycat you. You will say a simple word four times and they'll repeat it.

TEACHER—Dog, dog, dog, dog.
CHILDREN—Dog, dog, dog, dog.
TEACHER—Cat, cat, cat, cat.
CHILDREN—Cat, cat, cat, cat.

NOW, INSTEAD of words, the class will copycat actions.

TEACHER—Claps four times, *clap-clap-clap-clap.*
CHILDREN—*Clap-clap-clap-clap.*

NOW, TEACH the song "I've Got a Rhythm." Explain that there will be a part in the song where they clap four times, just as they have been doing. Then, sing the song.

AFTER THE children have learned the song and can sing it comfortably you can begin to substitute other body actions for the handclapping—snap fingers four times, click tongues four times, jump into the air four times. Let the children take turns leading the actions and choosing which part of the body will move four times.

YOU MAY ALSO substitute other rhythm patterns. Examples:

SUBSTITUTE animal sounds and actions—dogs bark and wag their tails, elephants trumpet and wave their trunks, monkeys say "chee-chee" and jump from tree to tree, etc.

87

CLAP CLAP TAP TAP

PURPOSE—*Participation in a rhythm pattern.*

THIS IS a wonderful exercise in learning rhythm patterns and note values. Children will learn to remember the patterns very quickly. This is the basis for remembering songs and can be very useful in remembering other kinds of information.

TEACHER SAYS, "Do what I do," and claps three times.

Do what I do
Clap   clap   clap (Clap hands, do not say the words)

Do what I do
Clap   clap   clap

Do what I do
Clap   clap   clap

Clap   clap   clap   clap   clap

AFTER THE children have learned this and can do it easily, you can add new rhythms. However, remember to always end with the original rhythm pattern.

Tap   tap   tap   (Tap hands on top of head or rhythm stick on table)

Do what I do
Tap   tap   tap

Do what I do
Tap   tap   tap
Tap   tap   tap   tap   tap
Clap   clap   clap   clap   clap

ALSO, ADD 3/4 time—left hand is "one," right hand is "two-three." Play this pattern: "one, two, three," left, right, right. You're playing 3/4 time, or "waltz time."

VARIATIONS—Snap fingers
                    Tap toes
                    Wiggle hips
                    Click tongues

PAPER GAME

PURPOSE—*Awareness of sound in everyday life.*

CHILDREN LOVE to make sounds with paper. I'm not sure why, but this game has always been a favorite with my children.

HOW MANY different kinds of sounds can you make with paper?

Crunch it   Tear it   Shake it   Cut it
Fan with it   Run fingers on it while it's held in the air

HERE ARE some games you can play with the paper sounds.

PAPER MUSIC GAME

CHOOSE A simple song or nursery rhyme that everyone knows. Let's use "Farmer in the Dell" as an example. For each line of the song, use a different paper sound.

> The farmer in the dell *(crunch paper)*,
> The farmer in the dell *(shake paper)*,
> Hi, ho, the derry-o, *(tear paper)*
> The farmer in the dell. *(run fingers on paper)*

SAY THE song and let the children make the paper sounds at the same time. After they can do it pretty well, make the paper sounds only and just mouth the words. Divide the class into four parts and assign one line to each group. Have them make the sound and say their line at the same time. Now, have them make the sound and just mouth the words.

SOUND GAME

PICK TWO paper sounds—for example, crunch and tear. Do them over and over until the children are familiar with them. The children hide their eyes while teacher makes the sound. The children have to guess the sound.

WHAT DO YOU LIKE ABOUT HALLOWEEN?

Words & Music
Miss Jackie Weissman

What do you like a - bout Hal - lo - ween?

What do you like a - bout Hal - lo - ween?

Solo: I like the (ghosts). *Group:* He likes the (ghosts).

Group: That's what we like a - bout Hal - lo - ween.

WHAT DO YOU LIKE ABOUT HALLOWEEN?

PURPOSE—*Teaching sequence.*

HALLOWEEN is an exciting holiday for children. Ask the children what ideas Halloween reminds them of.

YOU WILL probably get these answers:

        Witch   Ghost   Monsters   Bats
        Black cat   Costumes   Trick or treat

EVERYONE sings the song "What Do You Like About Halloween?" One child sings, "I like the _____ " (for example, "ghosts"). Then, everyone sings together, "He likes the ghosts. That's what we like about Halloween."

NOW, PICK a second child, who sings, "I like the _____" (for example, "witch"). The class echoes, "She likes the witch." After the second child and the class have sung their parts, the first child sings his part again.

NOW, PICK a third child and proceed as above. With each succeeding verse add a solo part. You'll soon have a kid's version of Gilbert and Sullivan in your own classroom.

AFTER THE children learn their parts and how to sing the song, substitute sounds for the names of the characters. Sing, "I like the *(make sound)*." The children repeat, "He likes the *(make sound)*."

MAKE UP other versions for other holidays. This song can be used all year round.

EVERYBODY HAS A HAPPY FACE

Words & Music
Miss Jackie Weissman

2. Everybody has a smiley smile,
   Everybody has a smiley smile,
   Everybody has a smiley smile,
   Every (clap) body.

3. Everybody has a tappin' foot,

4. Everybody has a snappin' hand

5. Everybody has a giggle laugh,

EVERYBODY HAS A HAPPY FACE

PURPOSE—*Response to a rhythm pattern.*

THIS IS a song that can be sung any time of the day. You can make up words to fit whatever activity the class is doing. It has a very definite rhythm pattern, which makes it easy to learn, and it is an excellent song for using rhythm sticks.

FIRST, TEACH the song to the children by singing it over and over. It is an easy song to learn and they will know it by about the fourth or fifth time. What word does each line start with? "Everybody." That's right.

SING THE song in various ways. First, sing "everybody" in a great BIG voice and the rest of the song in a normal voice. Then, sing "everybody" in a little tiny voice and the rest of the song in a normal voice.

NEXT, CLAP the word "everybody" and sing the rest of the words. Then, sing "everybody" and clap the rest of the song. Think of other actions instead of clapping—stamping feet, jumping up in the air, beating chest, clicking tongue.

GIVE EACH child one or two rhythm sticks. Substitute hitting the rhythm sticks on the floor (or on one another) for the clapping parts. Hit the sticks loudly and softly—hit them together, over your head, behind your back, or rub them against each other. (This works well with fluted sticks, if you have them.)

TALK ON THE BEAT

PURPOSE—*Response to a rhythm pattern.*

THE OBJECT of this game is to be able to say a word on the beat. This is not easy at first, but it is a wonderful rhythm lesson. The rhythm must be steady and ongoing.

CHOOSE A subject that the class has in common. For example, things around the house. Talk about all the things people have in their homes— doors, rooms, refrigerator, stove, yard, mother, father, etc. Each child gets to have his or her own exclusive thing. Go around the room and ask each child to tell you the name of the thing they are thinking of. (It's okay for two children to have the same word.) When each child has his or her own thing, you're ready to play the game.

SIT IN A circle with the class. Clap your hands and count to four with a steady rhythm. Have the children join in. You should be clapping and counting at the same time.

One	Two	Three	Four
clap	*clap*	*clap*	*clap*

TELL THE children that this time, instead of saying the word "four," you are going to say the name of a thing in your house. For example, "One, two, three, stove." Practice this several times. Now, tell the children that they are going to take turns in the circle. Each child, one at a time, will get to say the name of his or her thing instead of saying "four." The idea here is for the teacher to keep counting—"one, two, three"—and on "four" someone will give the name of his or her thing.

IF A CHILD misses the beat, keep counting and give as many chances as are necessary. If a child is having trouble, say the word with the child. This is a game at which every child should succeed, and is a very good way to recall experiences.

VARIATIONS—Some other ideas: things at the circus, animals on the farm, things that have wheels.

Say the name of the thing on the first count of four. (It's much harder to say the name on the count of two or three, but if your children are older you might try it.)

CHASE THE SOUND

PURPOSE—*To develop auditory discrimination.*

THE FOLLOWING two games involve listening to and locating sounds. In the first game, the child listens and identifies where the sound is. In the second game, the child must identify where the sound is and then go to it.

GAME 1

THE CHILDREN sit in a row. Teacher explains that she is going to make a drum sound in different parts of the room. The children close their eyes and, when the drum sounds, they must say where the sound is. It is sufficient for the answers to be in front, behind, close, far, up, down, on the side, etc.

A DRUM IS the proper instrument for this game.

GAME 2

THE CHILDREN are again seated in a row. One of the children is selected to go to a place in the room and make a sound. The other children have their eyes closed. One of the children is chosen to "go to" the sound. (Since the child's eyes will be closed, teacher should guide the child so nobody is hurt.)

VARIATIONS—If the sound is soft, the child moves very softly.

If the sound is loud, the child moves loudly (stomping, marching, etc.).

INSTRUMENTS

RHYTHM INSTRUMENTS teach many kinds of skills. Playing an instrument is like making a machine go. You are attached to your body, so when you clap your hands or tap your feet you are using yourself. When you play an instrument you are using an additional developmental skill.

THE USE OF INSTRUMENTS develops fine motor and listening skills and instills a sense of pride in being able to control the instrument being played.

TELL A TALE OF RHYTHM

PURPOSE—*To develop imagination and listening skills.*

CHILDREN WILL use their natural sense of rhythm along with their imagination during this activity. The only instruments needed are rhythm sticks.

TAP RHYTHM sticks on different surfaces. Notice that the sounds are different. Have the children identify what they think the sound reminds them of. For example:

Desk	sounds like	raindrops
Floor	sounds like	hammer
Window	sounds like	woodpecker
Metal	sounds like	echoes in a tunnel
Shoe	sounds like	faucet dripping

AFTER YOU HAVE identified many sounds, the next step is to attach rhythm patterns to each idea. For example:

Raindrops
Hammer
etc.

THIS IS how the game is played: teacher taps a rhythm on the appropriate surface. The children identify the sound. Go through all of the rhythms you have discussed and have the children identify them. Then, have the children close their eyes. One child goes to a surface and taps a rhythm. The other children try to guess what the surface is from either the sound or the rhythm.

TAKE A familiar story and find parts in it where rhythm sticks can make sound effects. Teacher tells the story and the children make the rhythm stick sound effects. For example: "Goldilocks was walking through the forest when it began to (rhythm for raindrops). She came upon a little house and (sound for knocking on the door)."

USE YOUR imagination and the children will use theirs.

TWINKLE, TWINKLE, LITTLE STICK

PURPOSE—*Imitating rhythms.*

SING TO the tune of "Twinkle, Twinkle, Little Star."

> Twinkle, twinkle, little stick;
> Some are thin and some are thick.
> When I hold you in my hand
> I pretend I'm in the band.
> Twinkle, twinkle, little stick.
> I'm so glad I know this trick.

GIVE EACH child one rhythm stick. As teacher sings the song with the children, the whole class keeps time to the music, four beats to each line. When the song is finished, teacher beats the same simple rhythm on the floor— ♩ ♩ ♩ ♩ . The children imitate the teacher with the same rhythm — ♩ ♩ ♩ ♩ . Teacher explains that this was the same rhythm used in the song.

HERE ARE some other rhythms:

(One half note and two quarter notes)

(Four eighth notes and two quarter notes)

(Two quarter notes, two eighth notes and
    one quarter note)

PRACTICE THE various rhythms with the class. The children will quickly catch on and will love the activity.

ASK FOR a volunteer leader, who gets to choose the rhythm and lead the class. Each child should get a turn to be the leader.

HIT THE STICKS in various locations—in front, in back, on the side, alternating sides, alternating back and forth. Also try loud and soft, fast and slow, etc.

RHYTHM STICK SOUNDS

PURPOSE—*Awareness of loud and soft.*

THIS GAME teaches the basic musical concept of loud and soft. The children have been making loud and soft noises all their lives, but they may not yet understand the concept.

TAKE OUT one rhythm stick and demonstrate the game this way: hit the stick loudly three times on the floor, saying "LOUD, LOUD, LOUD" as you hit the stick. Next, hit the stick softly on the floor, saying "soft, soft, soft" as you do so. Repeat this game as many times as you think is necessary to illustrate the concept.

NOW, HAVE the class say the words with you—first, "LOUD, LOUD, LOUD" and then "soft, soft, soft." Repeat this several times.

NEXT, ALTERNATE your sound patterns—three louds, then three more louds, then three softs, then three more softs. Go slowly enough so that the children can identify loud or soft without your help.

PASS OUT rhythm sticks to the class. Have the children hit the sticks as you direct, "LOUD, LOUD, LOUD" and "soft, soft, soft." Alternate your patterns, as above. If a child needs help producing a loud or soft sound, guide the child by putting your hand on the child's hand.

NOW, HAVE the children take turns hitting their sticks loudly or softly as the other children guess which sound is being made.

YOU CAN vary this game by changing the object producing the sounds (use tone blocks, wooden spoons, a drum and drumsticks, etc.) and by changing the surface that is being hit—chairs, blackboard, tin pot, etc.

RHYTHM EXPRESSES FEELINGS

PURPOSE— *To show how feelings can be expressed with different musical instruments.*

SOME CHILDREN are shy and do not like to express themselves verbally. The following game is a good one that affords the opportunity to express feelings without speaking. This game works best with groups of five or six.

TAKE OUT your rhythm instruments, the more the better. Xylophone, maracas, tone blocks, bells, rhythm sticks—all work well with this game.

ILLUSTRATE each of the instruments for the children. Play each one and discuss the special sound each one makes. Discuss how fast playing makes you feel a certain way and how slow playing makes you feel another way. Bells have a happy sound while a xylophone may suggest movement, up and down, fast and slow.

SEAT THE class in a circle, teacher included. Say, "When I was on my way to school today, I felt _____." Pick an instrument and play it to express your feelings.

NEXT, SAY to the first child, "Mary Ann, how did you feel on the way to school today?" Mary Ann then chooses an instrument and illustrates how she felt.

AFTER ALL of the children have expressed how they felt with their rhythm instruments, ask other questions. "How do you go home from your school? Do you walk, run, hop or skip?" "What is your favorite holiday?"

THIS IS a wonderful exercise in creativity and teaches the concept that feelings can be expressed in many ways besides speech. In fact, this is the basis for much art, such as music and painting.

THE AUTOHARP—
A TEACHER'S FRIEND

PURPOSE—*To investigate an invaluable teacher's aid.*

THE AUTOHARP is an inexpensive, easy-to-learn instrument that can be a valuable asset in the classroom. You do not need to be a skilled musician to learn to play the autoharp; in fact, practically anyone can learn to play simple songs after just a few minutes of practice.

THE AUTOHARP is also a sturdy instrument. The children can play it, too. Don't be afraid that they'll damage the instrument.

EXAMINE THE strings. You can see they are different lengths and thicknesses. How do the long strings sound? How about the short strings? As you pluck the strings, notice the vibrations. Notice that you can barely see the vibrations of the short strings but that it is fairly easy to see the vibrations of the long strings.

STRUMMING THE autoharp means to run your finger or a pick across all the strings. Do this a few times until you feel comfortable doing it. First do it fast, then slowly.

NOTICE THAT the autoharp has buttons. Each button has a letter on it. Play a C chord by pressing the C button with one hand and strumming the strings with the other hand. Continue to hold down the button as you strum the C chord over and over a few times. Now, go to the G button and repeat the process. Play the G chord over and over a few times.

NOW FOR the acid test: alternate the C and G chords over and over several times. Does it remind you of a song? It should, because you have just played a chord sequence that is common to many simple songs.

YOU MAY NOT realize it, but you have just learned to play the autoharp! With just a little more practice you'll be able to play many songs. It will make your classroom work easier and more enjoyable.

LET THE children join in the fun. Have one child come forward and strum while you play the chords. Have the child press the button while you strum. Let each child have a turn, then have the class sing a song while you accompany them on the 'harp.

MAKING MUSIC IN THE KITCHEN

Words & Music
Miss Jackie Weissman

I'm ma - king mu - sic in the kit - chen,

I'm ma - king mu - sic in the kit - chen. Lis - ten to the sound, the

kit - chen sound. Can you guess what it is?

MAKING MUSIC IN THE KITCHEN

PURPOSE—*Awareness of rhythms and sounds around us.*

PASS OUT various kitchen utensils—egg beaters, flour sifters, spoons, pots and pans, etc.

SING THE song "I'm Making Music in the Kitchen" and teach the class. After the class has learned the song, teacher sings it once through. Pick one of the utensils and hit it on the desk or floor. Pick one of the children to come forward and match the sound.

EACH CHILD in class gets to come forward and match your kitchen sound. Tell them to remember the sound for the game that is about to be played.

THE GAME—Children close their eyes and keep them closed. Teacher makes a sound with each of the kitchen objects. Teacher then selects one child to come forward, eyes open and match the sound. Each child has a turn and all the kitchen objects should be used.

AFTER THE children are familiar with the game, the teacher can be replaced with a child. The class then plays the game by themselves while teacher monitors. Suggest variations, such as combining utensils to make new sounds. Hit the utensils rapidly against one another, then slowly. Have the children make their own suggestions.

PIANO GAMES

PURPOSE—*Exploring a musical instrument.*

HERE IS a finger play about the piano.

> Here's the hammer *(make a fist with one hand)*
> Here are the strings *(spread fingers of other hand)*
> Hit them together *(hammer hand hits string hand)*
> The piano sings *(keep hitting hammer hand on string hand)*

YOU CAN teach a lot about a piano even if you can't play it. Inspect the keys. They are made of ivory. Where does ivory come from? What does a bird's song sound like? *(Play the extreme right-hand keys very lightly.)* What does the thunder sound like? *(Play the extreme left-hand keys loudly.)*

FIND MIDDLE C on the piano. You can play a simple scale by playing middle C and the seven white keys to the right. Play them up, then play them down. Notice the black keys in between? These are half-steps. If you play them in order with the scale you've just learned, it's a chromatic scale.

NOTICE THE pedals near the floor? The pedal on the left softens the tone being played. The right pedal sustains the note. You can do "magic" on the piano: play a note while pressing down on the right pedal, then take your finger off the note (but keep your foot on the pedal). The tone will continue to play! When you let the children in on your "secret," they will all want to try it.

USE YOUR piano, if you have one. Children will be fascinated by it.

FOUR STICK GAMES

PURPOSE—*Fun with rhythm sticks.*

1. POP GOES THE WEASEL

SING THE song and hit your sticks on *pop.* Have the children hide their sticks behind their backs until it's time to *pop.*

2. ONE, TWO, THREE, FOUR

HIT STICKS in rhythm to the following poem:

> *One, two, three, four,*
> *Who's that knocking on my door?*
> *Five, six, seven, eight,*
> *Hurry up, I just can't wait.*

VARY THE manner in which you lead the rhythm. First, hit sticks on every beat, four beats to each line. Next, hit sticks on every other beat (on the first and third beats of each line, then the second and fourth beats of each line), etc. Let the children take turns being the leader and choosing the rhythm pattern and the surface to be hit.

3. FOLLOW THE BEAT

USE A metronome or a timer with this game. Have the children hit their sticks on the floor in time to the beat. Vary the speed of the timer. Make up a story to go with the various speeds. Fast speeds can be animals scampering through the woods. Slow speeds can be bears and elephants lumbering through the trees.

4. MARY MACK

DIVIDE THE class into twos so that each child has a partner. The partners sit facing each other, each with two rhythm sticks. One child holds the sticks in front of himself; the second child uses her sticks to hit the first child's sticks on the repeated words: "Miss Mary Mack"—hit sticks— "Mack"—hit sticks—"Mack"—hit sticks—"All dressed in black"—hit sticks—"black"—hit sticks—"black"—hit sticks. Sing the song all the way through, then have the partners switch roles.

GAMES FOR PERCUSSION

PURPOSE—*An introduction to various other rhythm instruments.*

RHYTHM STICKS have been dealt with extensively in other parts of this book, along with several other rhythm instruments, such as bells. Here are a few games for rhythm instruments not treated elsewhere in the book.

DRUMS

TEACHER PLAYS a certain rhythm on a drum. The children come forward one at a time and imitate the rhythm. (Always play the same rhythm, because repetition will teach the rhythm.) Play simple rhythms like:

ANOTHER DRUM GAME

TEACHER STRIKES the drum in a certain way. Notice that if you strike the drum around the edges it has a certain "high" sound. If you strike it in the center it has a "low" sound. The children have to say their names in the same way you strike the drum. Strike the drum in a "high" tone; the child you call on has to say his or her name in a "high" voice. Strike the drum in a "low" tone, and the child you call on must say his or her name in a low voice. This is a wonderful listening skill exercise.

TONE BLOCKS

THESE ARE very subtle instruments—whenever you strike them, you get a different tone. They're perfect for teaching advanced tone discrimination. Strike a certain tone pattern on the block. The child tries to imitate it. (Do not use a rhythm pattern or the exercise will be too difficult for young children.) Use a simple pattern—1, 2, 3, 4—and no more than two tones, at least in the beginning. As the children begin to learn the exercise, use more tones.

HANDBELLS, MARACAS, TAMBOURINES

THESE ARE similar instruments. With each, you can vary the speed, intensity and rhythm to play auditory discrimination games, as above. Give each child in the class either a handbell or a maraca. The teacher plays a pattern and the class tries to imitate it.

CAN YOU KAZOO?

PURPOSE—*To introduce children to a simple musical instrument.*

THE KAZOO is the simplest of instruments that plays a melody. The music is produced by humming the melody into the kazoo, causing the vibrating membrane to produce a musical sound. Because of its simplicity, the kazoo is a valuable aid in teaching young children about musical instruments. (Note: for health reasons, be sure that each child has his or her own individual kazoo. It's a good idea to label the kazoos with the children's names so they don't get mixed up.)

ASSEMBLE THE "orchestra" by dividing the class into two parts. Play a simple tune like "Mary Had a Little Lamb" with each of the two groups playing alternate lines.

CREATE YOUR own marching band by having the children line up two or four abreast and march around the room playing "Yankee Doodle" or "Oh, Susannah."

LET HALF the class play rhythm sticks while the other half plays kazoos.

PLAYING SONGS YOU KNOW

PURPOSE—*Enlarging one's repertoire of easy-to-play pieces.*

IF YOU PLAY a piano, autoharp, guitar or any other instrument that can be chorded, you can easily accompany yourself and the children to virtually hundreds of songs. On this page are songs that use only two or three chords. Good luck!!

TWO-CHORD SONGS

Who's That Tapping
  at the Window?
B'ym Bye
Jim Along Josee
Old Joe Clark
Bought Me a Cat
Hush Li'l Baby
Eensy Weensy Spider
Sally Go Round the Sun
This Old Man
Skip to My Lou
Paw Paw Patch
Hushabye
Cherry Tree Carol
Hey Liley Liley
Grand Old Duke of York
Mary Had a Little Lamb
Mulberry Bush
Oh Where, Oh Where Has My
  Little Dog Gone?
Looby Loo
Humpty Dumpty
Billy Boy
Hunting We Will Go
Alouette
Aunt Rhody
Clementine
Did You Ever See a Lassie?
Polly Wolly Doodle
Little Dreidle
Frere Jacques
Wheels on the Bus
London Bridge

THREE-CHORD SONGS

Coming Round the Mountain
Frog Went a-Courtin'
Jimmy Crack Corn
Put Your Finger in the Air
Happy Birthday
So Long, It's Been
  Good to Know You
This Land Is Your Land
Oh, Susannah
Twinkle, Twinkle, Little Star
ABC Song
Yankee Doodle
If You're Happy and You Know It
Bingo
Camptown Races
John Brown's Body
Kum Ba Yah
The Magic Penny
Little Brown Jug
Aiken Drum
Baa Baa Black Sheep
I Had a Rooster

110

MULTI-CULTURAL RHYTHM EXPERIENCES

IT HAS ALWAYS fascinated me that babies all over the world make the same sounds in their development—ma-ma and da-da are universal.

THERE IS also a "universal" song that all children sing all over the world. It is referred to as the "Ur" song. You know it—"Ring Around the Rosy," "You're a Dirty Robber," etc. The famous minor third.

AS YOUNG children experience songs and rhythms that children in other parts of the world enjoy, they soon discover and appreciate the similarities as well as the dissimilarities.

CHE CHE KOOLAY

PURPOSE—*Imitating rhythms.*

THIS IS a rhythm game from the country of Ghana, in Africa. The words are mainly nonsense syllables. First, say the words to the children.

> Che *(pronounced "chay")* che koolay
> Che che koolay
> Che che kofeesa
> Che che kofeesa
> Ko fee salanga
> Ko fee salanga
> Ca ca shi langa
> Ca ca shi langa
> Koom ma dye *(pronounced "deay")* day
> Koom ma dye day.

TEACHER SAYS one part and the children imitate her. Go very slowly at first.

TEACHER—Che che koolay
CHILDREN—Che che koolay
TEACHER—Che che kofeesa
CHILDREN—Che che kofeesa

Continue until the chant is finished.

TEACHER NOW uses rhythm sticks to beat out the rhythm. First say the words and hit the sticks on the floor at the same time. Next, have the children do this with you.

NOW, TRY hitting the rhythm and having the children echo the rhythm with their sticks. (REMEMBER—no words, just beat the rhythm.)

HERE IS the rhythm:

> Che che koolay—2X
> Che che kofeesa—2X
> Ko fee salanga—2X
> Ca ca shi langa—2X
> Koom ma dye day—2X

MY HAT IT HAS THREE CORNERS

German Folk Song

My hat it has __ three corn - ers, _____ three
corn - ers has my hat. _____ And had it not __ three
corn - ers, _____ it would not be my hat. _____

MY HAT IT HAS THREE CORNERS

PURPOSE—*Developing muscle coordination.*

ON THE WORD "hat," touch your head. On the word "three," hold up three fingers. On the word "corners," raise your elbow into the air.

THIS OLD German folk song is very popular with young children. The idea of the song is to first sing it and then begin to substitute actions instead of singing the words.

SING THE song through, with the words. The second time, do the actions for "hat" (and sing the word). The third time, do the actions for both "hat" and "three" (and sing the words). The fourth time, do the actions for "hat," "three" and "corner" while singing the words.

IT IS IMPORTANT to sing the words *and* do the actions, as this game is developmental. After the children can sing the song and do the actions comfortably, you can begin to leave out the words and only do the actions—first leave out "hat," then "hat" and "three," then "hat," "three" and "corners."

THE MENEHUNE SONG

Words: *Miss Jackie* Weissman
Jerry Maloney

Music: *Miss Jackie* Weissman

THE MENEHUNE SONG

PURPOSE—*To introduce children to mythical creatures.*

MENEHUNE ELVES are mythical creatures who inhabit the caves of Hawaii. They are happy little people who sleep all day and come out only after nightfall. Their greatest pleasure is to surprise "big people" by doing work for them in the middle of the night. As soon as daylight comes the Menehunes disappear back into their caves, where they spend the day sleeping and eating bananas and shrimp. Folklore says that if you look very carefully at the mist on the mountain at night you may be able to see the Menehunes—and, if you're very, very quiet, you may be able to hear them singing.

HAVE THE children join hands as they sing the song. On the "tip, tip, toe" part they can tiptoe together. In the second verse they can make hand gestures and "put things back where they belong." In the third verse they can tiptoe again; in the fourth verse they can tiptoe backward, "disappear" and, in the final line, "Bananas, shrimp and _____," they should fill in their own word with something that's fun to say—macaroni, spaghetti, ice cream, pizza.

HEVENU SHALOM A'LEYCHEM

Israel: Greeting Song

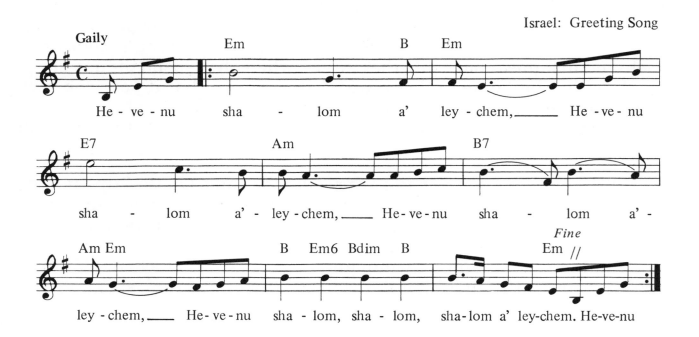

He - ve - nu sha - lom a' ley - chem,_____ He - ve - nu sha - lom a' ley - chem,_____ He - ve - nu sha - lom a' - ley - chem,_____ He - ve - nu sha - lom, sha - lom, sha - lom a' ley - chem. He - ve - nu

118

HEVENU SHALOM A'LEYCHEM

PURPOSE—*To teach "welcome" in a new language.*

THIS SONG is an Israeli greeting song. The word "shalom" has three meanings: hello, goodbye and peace.

THE CHILDREN should always sing this song enthusiastically, with the last two "shaloms" SHOUTED out. The rhythm suggests marching. Have the children form a circle and march around as they sing the song. Next, have each child take a partner, hold each other's hands and march around the circle together, singing.

THIS SONG can also be sung with clapping hands, stamping feet, snapping fingers, etc. This is a wonderful song for waiting in line, traveling on the bus and beginning the day.

THE ZULU WARRIOR

Traditional

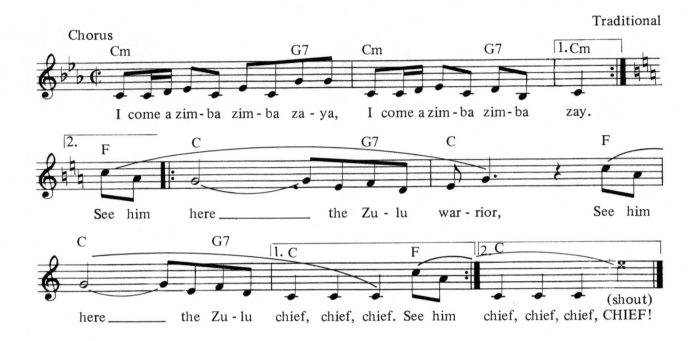

I come a zimba zimba zaya,
I come a zimba zimba zay.
I come a zimba zimba zaya,
I come a zimba zimba zay.
See him here the Zulu warrior,
See him here the Zulu chief, chief, chief.
See him here the Zulu warrior,
See him here the Zulu chief, chief, chief.

120

ZULU WARRIOR

PURPOSE—*Developing rhythm in young children.*

THIS TRADITIONAL African song is fun to sing. The strong underlying rhythm is easily learned and children will respond immediately.

SIT IN a circle and sing the song. Teacher can beat a hand drum if desired and the children can beat their hands or sticks on the floor to the underlying rhythm.

ONE CHILD is chosen to be the chief, who goes into the circle and dances to the music whatever way the child thinks a chief would dance. On the last "chief" the child in the circle jumps high in the air as the children shout out the word.

THE CHIEF then chooses a new chief to go into the circle and the old chief sits in the circle with the rest of the class.

OLDER CHILDREN like to sing this song as a two-part round. You can vary the rhythm expression on the chorus. You might want to clap hands, snap fingers or change the sound of your voice. (When I learned this as a child we sang the first two "chiefs" in the last line very softly and then we shouted out the last one.)

THIS SONG offers many introductory possibilities for learning about African culture.

HANUKAH

Adapted
Miss Jackie Weissman

Jewish Folk Song

Han - u - kah, Han - u - kah, hap - py hol - i - day.

Chil - dren sing, chil - dren dance, can - dles burn a - way.

Han - u - kah, Han - u - kah, tops spin round and round.

Spin spin spin spin spin spin what a love - ly sound.

HANUKAH

PURPOSE—*To enlighten children about a Jewish holiday.*

HANUKAH IS a celebration of the defeat of the Syrian Army by Judah Maccabee in the year 165 B.C. This defeat gave the Jews freedom to worship as they believed and to rebuild their temple in Jerusalem. The holiday is meaningful to all people because it represents freedom.

THE HOLIDAY is celebrated for eight days to commemorate the "miracle" of the eternal light: though the people of Jerusalem thought there was only enough oil to burn in the temple for one day, it burned a full eight. During the holiday people give presents, eat special foods and hold parties.

THIS SONG is lovely to use rhythm instruments with. At the end of every four measures there is a pause where triangles, toneblocks and tambourines sound wonderful.

> Hanukah, Hanukah, happy holiday *(play the instruments one beat)*
> Children sing, children dance,
> Candles blaze away *(instruments, etc.)*

ON THE WORDS "Hanukah, Hanukah," children pretend to be tops* and spin around and around. On the words "Spin, spin, spin, spin, spin, what a lovely sound," the children make a *whooosh* sound with their voices and fall to the ground.

DIVIDE THE group into two parts—one part sings the song and plays the instruments, the other group can be the tops.

* The Hebrew word for "top" is *dreidle.*

THE LEPRECHAUN SONG

Words: *Miss Jackie* Weissman
Jerry Maloney
Music: *Miss Jackie* Weissman

1., 5. Out in the deep dark for - est,
2. Pat - rick Le - pre - chaun stood up
3. Pat - rick's shoes are stur - dy, strong

Un - der a tree so green Two lit - tle le - pre - chauns
And said, "My shoes are grand." "Oh Blar - ney," Mike said
And per - fect for a king. Mich - ael's shoes are

mak - ing shoes for the fair - y king and queen.
"My shoes are the fin - est in this land."
shi - ny bright and per - fect for the

queen. 4. The king and queen ar - rived just then and

saw their shoes of green. "B' - gor - rah and B' -

gosh," they said, "They're the fin - est I've ev - er seen."

THE LEPRECHAUN SONG

PURPOSE—*To teach children about an Irish myth.*

LEPRECHAUNS are mythical people who live in the forests of Ireland. They are wrinkled little old men who are very cranky. They live alone, far from the towns, and their main occupation is making shoes and boots for the *shees* (fairies) of Ireland. People often try to catch—or even just see—a leprechaun, but so far no one has been successful.

THIS SONG is meant just for fun, while exposing the children to the folklore of other countries. There are some fun words to learn—"blarney," "begorrah," "b'gosh"—and this is a good time to explain to the children that all countries have their myths: goblins, ghosts, leprechauns, tooth fairies and the like. You can also talk about "Snow White and the Seven Dwarfs" and other fairy tales. Explain that in olden days, before television, people would tell each other these stories for entertainment. People were superstitious then and nobody was really sure if these mythical creatures existed or not.

LEPRECHAUNS, elves and fairies are spoken of today as creatures of fun and mystery. You can explain that none of these mysterious creatures really exists.

THIS SONG is a creative dramatic song; the words lend themselves to being acted out.

SELF-ESTEEM

WHEN CHILDREN are expressing rhythm they feel in control of their environment. To develop self-esteem in a child is to help the child be in charge of his or her world.

RHYTHM EXPERIENCES give young children confidence in themselves, which in turn develops good self-concept.

I'M SO MAD

Words & Music
Miss Jackie Weissman

I'm so mad I could scream, I'm so mad I could scream.

I'm so mad, I'm real - ly mad, I could scream, I could scream, I could scream.

I'm so mad I could stomp, I'm so mad I could stomp.

I'm so mad, I'm real - ly mad, I could stomp, I could stomp, I could stomp.

I'm so sad I could cry
I'm so glad I could sigh.

I'M SO MAD

PURPOSE—*Identifying feelings with song.*

YOU WOULD be well advised to prepare the children for this song, since there's going to be a lot of screaming and you'll want to keep it under control.

TELL THE children that when you hold your hand in the air they should scream. When you point your finger toward the floor, they have to stop screaming.

SING THE song using the scream—they'll love it!

> I'm so mad I could scream *(kids scream)*
> I'm so mad I could scream *(kids scream)*
> I'm so mad, I'm really mad,
> I could scream, I could scream, I could scream! *(kids scream)*

ALSO, TRY this variation:

> I'm so glad I could sigh *(kids sigh)*
> I'm so glad I could sigh *(kids sigh)*
> I'm so glad, I'm really glad,
> I could sigh, I could sigh, I could sigh! *(kids sigh)*

THIS IS a good time to discuss feelings. How do the children feel when they're mad? sad? happy? afraid?

THIS SONG is open-ended; you can substitute words to make many, many versions. Try "I'm so scared I could shake" or "I'm so happy I could laugh."

(NOTE: I recommend the "scream" version for times when the class is getting edgy. It will relieve tension—for teacher, too! Or, sing the song on days when you cannot get outside to run off energy.)

LULLABYE

Words & Music
Miss Jackie Weissman

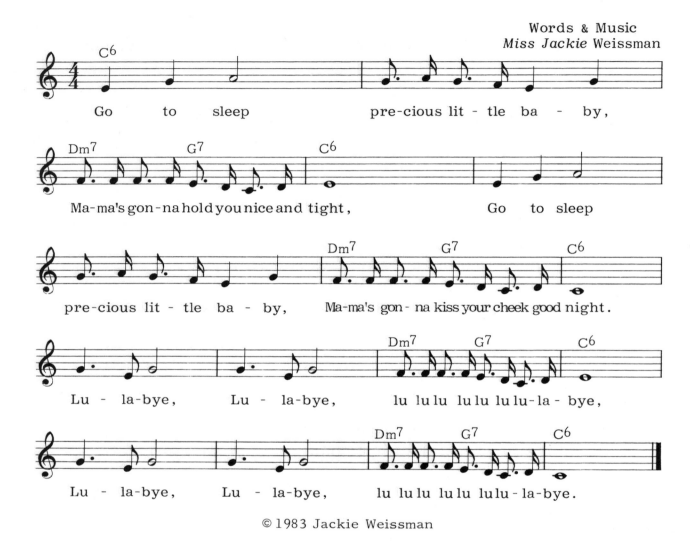

Go to sleep precious lit - tle ba - by,

Ma-ma's gon-na hold you nice and tight, Go to sleep

precious lit - tle ba - by, Ma-ma's gon - na kiss your cheek good night.

Lu - la-bye, Lu - la-bye, lu lu lu lu lu lu lu-la - bye,

Lu - la-bye, Lu - la-bye, lu lu lu lu lu lu lu-la-bye.

THIS song will be understood by all babies. Even if they do not understand the words of the song, the melody and rhythm immediately suggest that it is a "sleepy song."

ROCK the baby and sing the song. When you come to the words "lullabye" press the baby close to you and move around the room.

LULLABYE

PURPOSE—*Learning through play.*

CHILDREN LEARN through play. In order for adults to understand nurturing, they have had to experience it as a child.

ROCKING A baby not only nurtures the baby but also develops a feeling for rhythm.

LET THE CHILDREN pretend they are holding a baby in their arms. As they sing the song, let them gently rock the baby. Most of the children will easily relate to this because they often have babies at home.

ANOTHER WAY to rock a baby is to stand up and move slowly as you rock.

OH, JOHN THE RABBIT

Traditional

Oh, John the Rab - bit, Yes ma'am, Got a

might - y hab - it, Yes ma'am, Jum-ping in my gar - den,

Yes ma'am, Cut-ting down my cab - bage, Yes ma'am, My

sweet po - ta - toes, Yes ma'am, My fresh to - ma - toes,

Yes ma'am, And if I live, ___ Yes ma'am, To

see next fall, ___ Yes ma'am, I ain't gon-na have, ___

Yes ma'am, No cot-ton at all, Yes ma'am.

132

OH, JOHN THE RABBIT

PURPOSE—*To spark imagination.*

SING THE song and let the children make up their own vegetables. If you want to let them get silly, let them make up any kind of food—this makes for lots of laughter. This song is wonderful for developing self-esteem.

>   Oh, John the rabbit, yes ma'am,
>   Got a mighty habit, yes ma'am,
>   Talkin' 'bout his friends, yes ma'am.

THE CHILDREN now can make up things about each other—for example, "has a pretty smile, yes ma'am," "nice to everybody, yes ma'am," etc. Instead of singing "John," fill in with a child's name from the class.

NOW, HAVE the children form a circle. Whoever is the rabbit hops to another child and says something nice about that child. Then, the class incorporates that into the song.

RHYTHM IDEAS
FOR SONGS YOU KNOW

WE ALL KNOW many songs that were a part of our childhood. This chapter is meant to motivate you into thinking of new and creative rhythm ideas that you can use with songs that you already know.

I WOULD LIKE to suggest that you sit down and make a list of the songs that you know and I'm sure you will be amazed at the large number.

POP GOES THE WEASEL

PURPOSE—*Developing motor skills and loud/soft concepts.*

>All around the cobbler's bench
>The monkey chased the weasel.
>The cobbler laughed to see such fun.
>POP goes the weasel.

THIS SONG has many possibilities for developing skills in young children. Here are some ideas for games to use with this song.

1. Stoop down low to the ground. Sing the song and, on the word "pop," jump up into the air.

2. The children walk around in a circle while singing the song. On the word "pop" they fall to the ground.

3. One child is the monkey and one child is the weasel. As the rest of the class sings the song, the monkey and weasel chase each other around a chair. On the word "pop," one of the two children tries to get into the chair. The child that doesn't get into the chair gets to choose another child to take his or her place.

4. Sing all the words in a very soft voice until you come to "pop goes the weasel." Sing it in a loud, outside voice.

5. Sing the song and clap your hands at the same time. When you come to the last line, starting with "pop," stamp your feet and clap your hands. You can play this game using many body rhythms—snapping fingers, patting thighs, jumping, hopping, skipping, galloping, etc. It has a great many possibilities.

6. Use rhythm instruments on the word "pop." This presents great excitement for the children as they wait to play the instrument on the word "pop."

FARMER IN THE DELL

PURPOSE—*Developing creativity and rhythmic movement.*

> The farmer in the dell,
> The farmer in the dell,
> Hi, ho, the derry-o,
> The farmer in the dell.

THE CHILDREN form a circle. The child chosen to be the farmer stands in the middle. As the song is sung the children who form the circle walk as they sing. The farmer then chooses someone to be the wife. The two of them then walk around the circle with the class and choose the next child who could be the cow, the horse, etc.

YOU CAN change the subject matter to fit the kind of curriculum you are studying in your classroom. For example, "The Monkey at the Zoo." Then, whoever is the monkey gets to choose another animal. The monkey takes an elephant, the elephant takes a tiger, etc. This makes for a more exciting game because the children can pretend they are the animals and move and sound as they think the animals do.

ANOTHER VERSION of this could be "The Driver on the Bus." You can play the game the same way and figure out all the different things that could go on the bus. This is very appealing to a young child's imagination. The words would be:

> The driver on the bus,
> The driver on the bus,
> Hi, ho, the derry-o,
> The driver on the bus.

THREE SONGS YOU KNOW

PURPOSE—*Having fun with familiar songs.*

HERE WE GO ROUND THE MULBERRY BUSH

THE CHILDREN form two concentric circles. The outer circle faces inward, the inner circle faces outward. While singing the song, one circle goes clockwise, the other circle goes counterclockwise. When the song repeats, the directions are reversed.

OR—

TWO CHILDREN are selected to be the mulberry bush. The rest of the children join hands and form a circle around the bush. As they sing the song they move clockwise around the bush. When the song ends, two other children become the bush. Play the game until all children have had a chance to be the bush. (The children can hop, skip or run around the bush, too.)

THIS OLD MAN

PASS OUT four different kinds of rhythm instruments, in equal amounts—for example, rhythm sticks, tone blocks, bells and maracas. Each child has an instrument. Have the children play their instruments as follows:

> This old man, he played one *(rhythm sticks play)*
> He played knick knack on my drum *(tone blocks play)*
> With a knick knack paddywhack, throw the dog a bone *(bells play)*
> This old man came rolling home *(maracas play).*

NOW, HAVE the children play the song without singing, just playing the rhythm.

ARE YOU SLEEPING?

DIVIDE THE class into four groups. Each group claps the song in a different place. For example:

> Are you sleeping, are you sleeping, *(group one)*
> Brother John, brother John? *(group two)*
> Morning bells are ringing, morning bells are ringing, *(group three)*
> Ding, ding, dong, ding, ding, dong *(rhythm sticks play).*

THEN, HAVE the children stamp the song or play it with rhythm sticks. The groups can change parts until each group has played all the parts.

FOUR SONGS YOU KNOW

PURPOSE—*Fun activities to develop skills.*

SHE'LL BE COMIN' ROUND THE MOUNTAIN

> She'll be comin' round the mountain when she comes,
> She'll be comin' round the mountain when she comes,
> She'll be comin' round the mountain
> She'll be comin' round the mountain
> She'll be comin' round the mountain when she comes.

HAVE THE children sit in a circle, either on chairs or on the floor. One child is designated as the "runner." As the class sings the song, the runner runs around the outside of the circle. At the end of the song, on the word "comes," the runner stops behind one of the children. This child then becomes the runner, and the first runner sits with the group.

ANOTHER VERSION is to have the running child drop out of the group. Each child who gets to run drops out until there is only one child left. This child is the "winner," who gets to go first the next time the game is played.

MICHAEL, ROW THE BOAT ASHORE

THIS SONG, used in an open-ended way, has limitless possibilities. The original way to sing this is simply to sing "Michael, row the boat ashore, hallelujah," two times to the melody.

SUBSTITUTE phrases that develop the children's self-esteem and self-concept by having them say nice and pleasant things about one another. "Susie's dress is yellow and green, hallelujah," "Johnny has a great big smile, hallelujah," "It is fun to come to school, hallelujah." A variation is to have the children play rhythm sticks to the melody—while singing the song and then without singing the song.

HICKORY, DICKORY, DOCK

ON THE WORDS "Hickory, dickory, dock" the children clap three times in rhythm. On "the mouse ran up the clock" they "run" their hands up over their chests to their faces. On "the clock struck one" they hold up one finger. On "down he ran" they "run" their fingers from their heads down to their laps. Then, on the last "hickory, dickory, dock," they clap three more times in rhythm.

BAA, BAA, BLACK SHEEP

AS THE CHILDREN sing the song, have them imitate the sheep's voice. Have them do a simple exercise in rhythm: they raise their arms on the beat, first the right arm, then the left arm. On the second verse they put forward alternate feet—first the right, then the left.

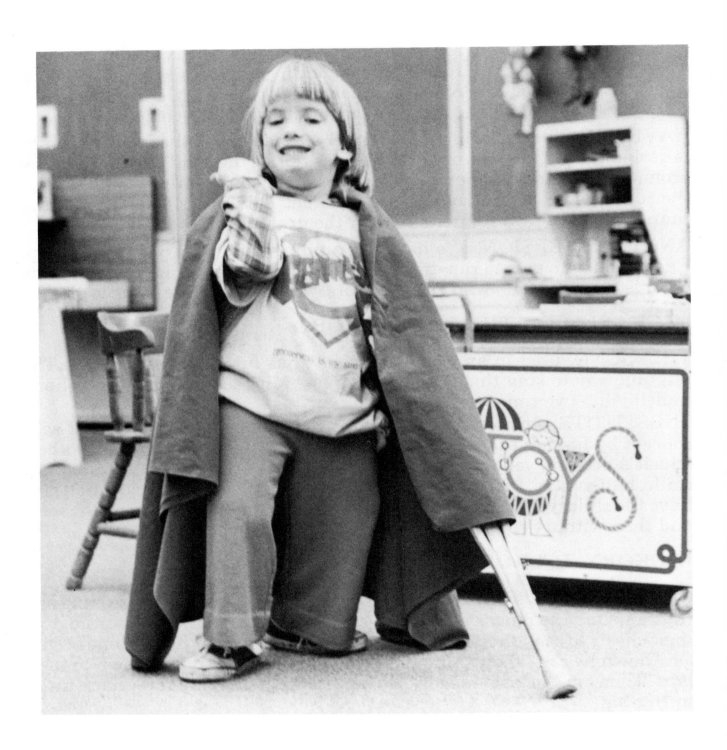

YANKEE DOODLE

PURPOSE—*Learning listening and language skills.*

ON THE TOP-TEN list of favorite songs for children, "Yankee Doodle" is usually number two or three. (Probably because of the word "macaroni"!)

THERE ARE many kinds of rhythm activities to do with "Yankee Doodle."

> Yankee Doodle went to town
> Riding on a pony;
> Stuck a feather in his cap
> And called it macaroni.
> Yankee Doodle, keep it up;
> Yankee Doodle Dandy.
> Mind the music and your step
> And with the girls be handy.
> WHOOOOOOOOOOA!!!

THE CHILDREN bounce up and down like they are on horses; when they come to "whooooooooooa," they pretend to pull the horse's reins back.

ANOTHER IDEA is to sing the first four lines in a very soft voice and the last four lines in a very big voice, then reverse the procedure. (The reversal is a good way to get children to quiet down!)

YANKEE DOODLE DANCE

The children form a circle and do these actions:

> Yankee Doodle went to town *(walk four steps into circle)*
> Riding on a pony; *(walk four steps back)*
> Stuck a feather in his cap *(step slide step to the right four times)*
> And called it macaroni *(step slide step to the left four times)*.

FOR THE NEXT four lines have the children pretend they're riding horses around the circle. At the end, stop and say "WHOOOOOOOOOOA!!!"

INDEX
First lines of songs

NOTE: A cassette tape of Miss Jackie singing all 26 songs from this book (in the exact order as they appear in the book) is available for $5.95. Write:

Miss Jackie Music Co.
10001 El Monte, Box RB
Overland Park, KS 66207

ABOUT MISS JACKIE

JACKIE WEISSMAN, better known as "Miss Jackie" to thousands of teachers, parents and children throughout the USA and Canada, is a children's concert artist, composer, educator, consultant, national columnist, recording artist and television personality.

SHE IS an adjunct instructor in Early Childhood Education at Emporia (Kansas) State University and a monthly contributor to the prestigious magazine for teachers, *The Instructor.*

MISS JACKIE is the author of seven books dealing with music and young children and has produced many workshop audio tapes and videotapes that are widely used for teacher training. She has recorded many of her own and others' songs. Please see page 144 for a partial listing of her books, records and cassette tapes.

FOR A FREE Miss Jackie catalog, please write:

Miss Jackie Music Co.
10001 El Monte, Box RB
Overland Park, KS 66207
(913) 381-3672

OTHER RECENT WORKS
BY MISS JACKIE

SNIGGLES, SQUIRRELS AND CHICKEN POX
40 Original Songs with Activities by Miss Jackie

THIS LONG-AWAITED collection of songs, most of which were originally in *The Instructor* magazine, contains such favorites as "Look Ma, No Cavities," "Ride, Sally, Ride," and the delightful "Sniggle Song."

LEARNING HAS never been such fun! Or so timely! From the fun-filled "King of the Jungle" to the thoughtful "Sing About Martin," each song is accompanied by suggested activities that will develop children's cognitive, motor and language skills while strengthening their self-concept and self-esteem.

THIS DELIGHTFUL 64-page musical treasure contains songs about animals, seasons, holidays, nursery rhymes and songs about our American heritage and traditions. Printed in clear, easy-to-read type with chords for piano, guitar and autoharp included, this book is only $8.95 at your school supply or teachers' store.

NEW!! NOW ALSO AVAILABLE AS A 33 RPM RECORD OR CASSETTE TAPE—17 of the songs from "Sniggles, Squirrels and Chicken Pox"! Miss Jackie, "Fred and the Kids" and a marvelous combo perform in a variety of musical moods. March to a stirring "Hooray for Mr. Lincoln," thrill to the spooky "Halloween," swing with the "Easter Bunny" and rock 'n' roll with "Old Mother Hubbard." The "kids" are charming in their ingenuousness and Miss Jackie is at her best in this setting—singing and having fun with children. Only $9.95 at your school supply or music store.

SONGS TO SING WITH BABIES

MISS JACKIE'S all-time best seller, this 64-page book full of songs with games and activities is the PERFECT GIFT! Chapter headings include Songs for Rocking and Nursing, Songs for Riding in the Car, Songs for Taking a Bath, Songs for Waiting for Meals, Songs for Laughing and Having Fun, Songs for Cuddling, Songs for Waking up and Songs for Getting Dressed. Three-, four- and five-year-olds love these songs and games, too. Charming illustrations and lots of child development information. Only $8.95!

For a FREE catalog of all Miss Jackie materials, write:

Miss Jackie Music Co.
10001 El Monte, Box RB
Overland Park, KS 66207
(913) 381-3672

144